Muslim
IN AMERICA

Other titles in the *Bias in America* series include:

Black in America
Hispanic in America
Jewish in America
LGBTQ in America

BIAS IN AMERICA

Muslim IN AMERICA

Leanne Currie-McGhee

ReferencePoint Press

San Diego, CA

© 2021 ReferencePoint Press, Inc.
Printed in the United States

For more information, contact:
ReferencePoint Press, Inc.
PO Box 27779
San Diego, CA 92198
www.ReferencePointPress.com

ALL RIGHTS RESERVED.
No part of this work covered by the copyright hereon may be reproduced or used in any form or by any means—graphic, electronic, or mechanical, including photocopying, recording, taping, web distribution, or information storage retrieval systems—without the written permission of the publisher.

LIBRARY OF CONGRESS CATALOGING-IN-PUBLICATION DATA

Names: Currie-McGhee, L. K. (Leanne K.), author.
Title: Muslim in America / by Leanne Currie-McGhee.
Description: San Diego, CA : ReferencePoint Press, Inc., 2021. | Series: Bias in America | Includes bibliographical references and index.
Identifiers: LCCN 2020016117 (print) | LCCN 2020016118 (ebook) | ISBN 9781682828991 (library binding) | ISBN 9781682829004 (ebook)
Subjects: LCSH: Muslims--United States--Social conditions--Juvenile literature. | Muslims--Civil rights--United States--Juvenile literature. | United States--Ethnic relations--Juvenile literature. | Muslims--United States--Juvenile literature. | Islam--United States--Juvenile literature.
Classification: LCC E184.M88 C874 2021 (print) | LCC E184.M88 (ebook) | DDC 305.6/90973--dc23
LC record available at https://lccn.loc.gov/2020016117
LC ebook record available at https://lccn.loc.gov/2020016118

CONTENTS

Introduction — 6
Thriving Against the Odds

Chapter One — 10
Islamophobia on the Rise

Chapter Two — 21
Growing Up Muslim

Chapter Three — 32
Hate Crimes

Chapter Four — 43
Political Impacts

Chapter Five — 54
Finding Their Place

Source Notes	65
Organizations and Websites	70
For Further Research	72
Index	74
Picture Credits	79
About the Author	80

INTRODUCTION

Thriving Against the Odds

"I'm an American. I'm an American and you're not. We're going to kill all of you, we're going to kill every one of you f---ing Muslims,"[1] shouted Amber Elizabeth Hensley at a group of young women in a Walmart parking lot in Fargo, North Dakota. The anger and racist words were her response to three women parking, in her mind, too close to her car. In 2017 Sarah Hassan, her sister Leyla Hassan, and their friend Rowda Soyan, all in their twenties, were the subjects of Hensley's abuse. Hensley hurled several other insults at the women, telling them they should not be in America.

The three women, who had immigrated from Somalia as refugees, were wearing traditional Muslim head scarves. This fact set them apart from "Americans" in Hensley's eyes. Sarah Hassan shot a video of the event for others to see how differently they are perceived. "I wanted everyone to see what happens to us every day," she says. "I was so scared."[2]

Who Are Muslims?

Hassan is one of the estimated 3.45 million Muslims living in the United States, according to a 2017 Pew Research Center study. A Muslim is a follower of the religion Islam, which is the fastest-growing religion in the world. The Islamic faith is predominant in countries in the Middle East but is also found throughout the world. In simple terms, followers of

Islam are monotheistic, which means they worship one all-knowing God, known in Arabic as Allah. Muslims believe that Muhammad was the final prophet and follow the teachings in the Koran, scripture that they believe was dictated to Muhammad by the angel Gabriel. However, there are many different branches of Islam that interpret the Koran differently, just as there are many different Christian denominations, for example, that interpret the Bible differently.

Muslims in America are a diverse group. For one, they are a mix of people who were either born in the United States or immigrated from other countries. The Pew Research Center also estimates that there are 2.15 million Muslim adults in the United States, and that 58 percent are immigrants. Many non-Muslim Americans associate Muslims with people of Arab descent, but this is not accurate. Even in America, Muslims have no dominant ethnic or racial heritage. According to a 2017

> "I'm an American. I'm an American and you're not."[1]
>
> —Amber Elizabeth Hensley, American woman who yelled at Muslim Americans

North Dakotan Amber Hensley spewed hateful, racist words at three young Somali refugees wearing traditional head scarves. Days later, at the urging of the Fargo police chief (left), Hensley (center) met with two of the women, Sarah Hassan and her sister Leyla Hassan. The three talked about their lives.

study done by the Institute for Social Policy and Understanding, American Muslims as a group are 25 percent black, 24 percent white, 18 percent Asian, 18 percent Arab, 7 percent mixed race, and 5 percent Hispanic.

Enduring Discrimination

What most Muslims in America have in common, aside from their faith, is that they face negative stereotypes and bias incidents from other Americans. In a 2017 Pew Research Center survey, Muslim Americans said that it has become harder to be Muslim in the United States in recent years. Seventy-five percent stated that there was discrimination against them in America, and 48 percent reported that, like Soyan and the Hassans, they had experienced at least one incident of discrimination in the past twelve months.

> "I wanted everyone to see what happens to us every day. I was so scared."[2]
>
> —Sarah Hassan, Muslim American woman confronted by Hensley

The perception of a growing bias against Muslims is supported by reports of hate incidents. From 2014 through June 2019, the Council on American-Islamic Relations (CAIR) recorded a total of 10,015 occurrences of anti-Muslim bias in America. And examples are still prevalent. In 2020, for instance, Nick VanDenBroeke, a Catholic priest in Minnesota, preached in a Sunday sermon that Islam was "the greatest threat in the world"[3] and urged his parishioners to oppose Muslim immigration into America. He later apologized for his words, but only after his words were reported in a local newspaper. Such comments, whether retracted or not, reveal a persistent prejudice against Muslim Americans that is often boldly spoken out loud.

Changing in the Future

Despite the bias, many Muslim Americans love the United States for what it offers. In fact, the 2017 Pew Research Center study found that 92 percent are proud to be Americans. Muslim Americans remain hopeful that they can change negative perceptions held by other Americans and do see progress. According to the Pew Research Center study, 49 percent of Muslim Americans report that someone has expressed support for them because of their religion in the past year, and 55 percent said that Americans in general are friendly toward US Muslims.

For Sarah Hassan, the incident with Hensley started as a terrible reminder of the bias that many people have against those of her faith. But she found signs of hope that Americans can get rid of the hatred and racism of some. Fargo police chief David Todd asked Hassan and her sister if they would meet with Hensley. They agreed. During this meeting, the women talked about the confrontation and found that, despite their differences, they had many things in common. At the meeting, Hassan showed pictures of and explained their culture to Hensley. Hensley explained that her dad was killed in Iraq, which is why she developed a bad view of Muslims. "We started talking and [Hensley] was like really, really sad, and then she told us she regrets everything she said to us,"[4] Hassan says. While in this case one person learned tolerance and shed some bias, the hope of Muslim Americans is that all Americans can work together to root out bias and end such discrimination.

CHAPTER ONE

Islamophobia on the Rise

As a middle school student, Saeda Sulieman discovered that going to classes while wearing a hijab, a head scarf worn by some Islamic women that covers the head and chest, can single her out and make her a target for discrimination. Sulieman, now a college student, recalls that she decided to wear the hijab in seventh grade because it made her feel closer to her religion. "Some people in my family don't [wear a hijab], and that's their decision, obviously, but I chose to because I felt like it made me closer to God, and it made me feel like a better person,"[5] Sulieman explains. However, in the first weeks of wearing it, she was called the Muslim slur "towelhead" by one classmate, and another called her a terrorist. Sulieman cried and told a teacher. The school quickly addressed the issue, and the comments stopped, but that could not take away the hurt she had felt. Still, Sulieman continued to wear the hijab at school because it was important to her.

Sulieman's experience is just one that many Muslim Americans deal with on a daily basis. Incidents like hers are the result of misinformation and misplaced anger against Muslim Americans that has risen in recent years. The overall rise of Islamophobia, fear of Muslims, in the United States followed from the September 11, 2001, terrorist attacks in America that left nearly three thousand people dead. Subsequent terrorist activities as well as the US war against terrorism fueled the negative feelings. However, the Muslims who perpetrated the 9/11 attacks and other terrorism believe in an extremist interpretation of Islam that is not shared by the majority of Muslims.

> "Some people in my family don't [wear a hijab], and that's their decision, obviously, but I chose to because I felt like it made me closer to God, and it made me feel like a better person."[5]
>
> —Saeda Sulieman, college studen

Smoke billows from the World Trade Center twin towers after a terrorist attack on September 11, 2001. The attack fueled hostility toward Muslim Americans and Muslims from other nations.

The Impact of Extremist Islam

Extremist Islam, or Islamism, is a view that democracy, individual liberty, and tolerance of different faiths go against Islamic principles. Additionally, extremist Islamists believe in a strict application of sharia law, which is a set of guiding moral principles derived from the teachings of the Prophet Muhammad. These individuals believe that a nation's governing and statutes should be based on the Koran and that anyone breaking these laws should face harsh punishments. Such views are unwelcome in most democratic countries like the United States because they conflict with principles of civil liberties, and most Muslim Americans—like most Muslims around the world—do not follow this narrow interpretation of Islam. According to a 2017 Pew Research Center survey, 73 percent of Muslim Americans say there is little to no support of Islamist extremism among Muslim Americans.

Despite the fact most Muslim Americans are not supportive of extremist interpretations of Islam, many Americans still view all Muslims as a dangerous threat, mainly because of the actions and beliefs of extremists. A 2019 poll by the Institute for Social Policy and Understanding found that its Islamophobia Index, which measures the level of fear of Muslims in America and ranges from 0 to 100, rose from 24 in 2018 to 28 in 2019. The index is based on surveys that ask Americans whether they agree or disagree with various statements, such as whether US Muslims are likely to engage in violence. The survey is of a representation of Americans of different religions and those who do not affiliate themselves with any religion. The results show that many non-Muslim Americans fear Muslim Americans simply because they follow a different religion—Islam—or because of a perception that the religion is connected to terrorism.

Contrasting Experience

Living with rising Islamophobia results in a daily life of extremes for Muslim Americans. Living in America is a positive experience for most Muslim Americans because of the opportunities and free-

Most Americans Believe US Muslims Experience Discrimination

A 2019 survey done by the Pew Research Center found that 82 percent of Americans believe that Muslims in the United States experience some or a lot of discrimination. Survey respondents expressed the view that Jews and evangelical Christians in the United States are also subjected to discrimination.

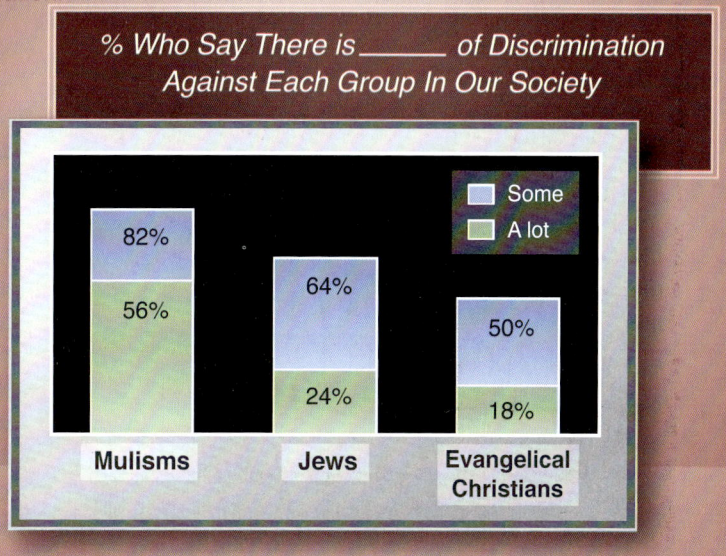

% Who Say There is _____ of Discrimination Against Each Group In Our Society

Group	Some	A lot
Mulisms	82%	56%
Jews	64%	24%
Evangelical Christians	50%	18%

Source: David Masci, "Many Americans See Religious Discrimination in U.S. – Especially Against Muslims," Pew Research Survey, March 17, 2019. www.pewresearch.org.

---

doms it provides. However, they also must deal with bias and discrimination. Dean Obeidallah, a Muslim American born in New Jersey to immigrant parents, became an attorney and then launched a career as a comedian. He currently has his own Sirius radio show. He has seen both sides of being a Muslim in America. "It truly is a tale of two experiences for Muslims today," Obeidallah writes. "On one hand, Muslims in America are seeing our greatest successes ever in ways that can be objectively measured. There are now three Muslims in Congress, the most ever. . . . Yet at the very same time there's a growing sense of unease and even fear that something horrible is waiting around the corner for us."[6]

> "There's a growing sense of unease and even fear that something horrible is waiting around the corner for us."[6]
>
> —Dean Obeidallah, radio show personality

Charities Fund Islamophobia

Charities are generally associated with positive actions—such as helping the homeless or providing for the poor. However, a 2019 report by the Council of American-Islamic Relations (CAIR) reveals that a significant amount of funding from charitable organizations goes to anti-Muslim organizations. The report states that from 2014 to 2016, over eight hundred largely mainstream charities gave money to thirty-nine anti-Muslim groups. CAIR found that these included major charitable foundations established by companies such as Fidelity Charitable and Schwab. Often people donated to these major foundations and did not know that some of the funding went to anti-Muslim groups.

The CAIR report says that nearly $125 million was given to such groups because they are registered as nonprofits and are not necessarily known for their anti-Muslim activities. ACT! for America, which is the largest anti-Muslim group in the country but is a registered nonprofit, was one recipient. "These anti-Muslim groups have more than a billion dollars in collective revenue that is used to advance an anti-Muslim agenda," says Zainab Arain, CAIR's national research and advocacy manager. "They lobby legislatures to pass anti-Muslim laws and policies, interfere in and falsify school curriculum and promote prejudicial and biased media content."

Quoted in Aysha Khan, "Over 1,000 Charity Groups Are Helping Fund Fringe Anti-Muslim Projects," *Oakland Press* (Troy, MI), May 27, 2019. www.theoaklandpress.com.

A main reason for that fear is the stereotypes held by many non-Muslims, including prevailing beliefs that Islam is a violent religion and is opposed to American ideals. These stereotypes include the beliefs that Muslims do not support democracy, are against women's rights, are anti-LGBTQ, and are proponents of violence. "The stereotype is that American Muslims are not able to be loyal to the United States because Islam pits them against the U.S," says Evelyn Alsultany, an associate professor in the Department of American Studies and Ethnicity at the University of Southern California in Los Angeles. "U.S. citizens are divided. . . . Islam is not seen as an American religion protected by the First Amendment right to freedom of religion, but rather as a religion of terrorism, anti-Americanism, anti-Semitism, misogyny, and homophobia."[7]

Studies support the idea that many non-Muslim Americans have difficulties accepting Muslims and hold negative views of them. A 2016 Pew Research Center study found that, while 49 percent of Americans said Islam is not more likely than other religions to encourage violence, 41 percent said it is more likely to encourage violence. Additionally, an April 2017 poll found that 50 percent of Americans polled said Islam is not a part of mainstream American society, and 44 percent believed that there is a natural conflict between Islam and democracy. Thus, many hold the belief that being a Muslim means an individual cannot truly support the United States or be part of its democratic society.

The irony is that the majority of Muslim Americans also worry about extremist Muslims and their actions. A 2017 Pew Research Center study found that about 82 percent of US Muslims say they are either very (66 percent) or somewhat (16 percent) concerned about extreme acts committed in the name of Islam around the world. Bisma Parvez, a Muslim American reporter, writes, "We want all Americans to know that we are scared too, just like you. We want good for our country, just like you. We want safety, just like you. We want a better life, just like you. And we want to be treated like one of you, because we too are American."[8]

Sources of Islamophobia in America

The most well-known terrorist act carried out by Islamist extremists is the 9/11 tragedy, in which radical Islamists, who were part of a terrorist group called al Qaeda, hijacked airliners and crashed them into the World Trade Center and the Pentagon. The plot was masterminded by Osama bin Laden, a Saudi Arabian man who believed in a militant form of Islam that would stand against Western aggression in the Middle East. He believed countries like Israel, Russia, and the United States were actively trying to destroy Islam. Under his direction in 1998, al Qaeda conducted attacks against US embassies in Africa that killed more than two hundred people, many of whom were innocent civilians. To Bin Laden, killing civilians in these countries was an acceptable form of jihad, a struggle or fight against the enemies of Islam. Even after Bin Laden's death in 2011, al Qaeda continues to preach a global jihad that insists Islam is in a fight for survival against Western secular beliefs and government aggression.

While these terrorist acts painted a bad image of foreign Muslims, other forms of terrorism committed by Muslim Americans convinced some Americans that any Muslim on US soil could be waiting to carry out such foul deeds. The Boston Marathon bombing in 2013, when two Muslim American brothers killed three people and injured several hundred, and the San Bernardino, California, shooting in 2015, when a Muslim American married couple killed fourteen people and injured twenty-two others in a mass shooting, proved to some that the jihad had come to America. Parvez writes:

> The sad fact is that many Americans are afraid of Muslims. After the terror attacks that have been associated with Muslims—9/11, the Boston Marathon, San Bernardino, to name a few—it's no surprise that Muslims are seen as bomb-hugging monsters. In movies, on TV, in the media, we are the bad guys. And if you are presented with the same image over and over again, it's bound to stick.[9]

But what many people do not realize is that, according to a study by the Anti-Defamation League, from 2008 to 2017, 71 percent of all terrorism-related fatalities in the United States were linked to domestic right-wing extremists. Only 26 percent of the killings were committed by Islamist extremists.

The Rise of Hate Crimes

After a terrorist event, anti-Muslim incidents spike in the United States. Following the 9/11 tragedy, Islamophobia skyrocketed

No Guns for Muslims

In 2016 Paul Chandler, the owner of Altra Firearms in rural Jackson Center, Pennsylvania, posted a sign on the door of his business and ran an ad in a local newspaper stating, "Please NO Muslims or Hillary Supporters—We do not feel safe selling to terrorists!" One local Pennsylvania paper refused to carry his ad, but a few others did carry it. Explaining the reasoning for the ban, Chandler said, "They want to destroy America, they want to destroy the American way of life." Other gun stores throughout the country have similar rules, claiming they can choose not to sell to people they believe are dangerous. Although the Civil Rights Act of 1964 prohibits discrimination based on religion at public accommodations, some owners and their legal representatives claim that gun stores are not bound by this regulation. Even the federal Bureau of Alcohol, Tobacco, Firearms and Explosives acknowledges that gun stores, as private businesses, have a good amount of leeway when deciding to whom to sell. "We have a responsibility not to sell weapons to people we think would use them in a crime or do something illegal with them," Chandler says. "I have to be honest with you—I do not feel safe selling weapons to Muslims." For Muslim Americans, such prejudice is just another instance of being denied respect as Americans.

Quoted in Kira Lerner, "Gun Store Runs Ad Saying It Won't Sell to Muslims, Clinton Supporters," ThinkProgress, October 28, 2016. https://thinkprogress.org.

as many Americans mistakenly equated Muslim beliefs with the radical, militant, and anti-American views of Bin Laden. Some of this fear turned into violence, and hate crimes ensued. For example, Craig Jennings and Jeffrey Lizotte were charged with a hate crime after they allegedly threw a Molotov cocktail onto the top of a store owned by Arab Americans in September 2001. The FBI reported that the number of anti-Muslim hate crimes rose from 28 in 2000 to 481 in 2001, after the September attacks.

Anti-Muslim organizations arose in response to 9/11 and the subsequent war on terror. These groups hold views about the alleged danger posed to America by the Muslim American community. Anti-Muslim organizations argue that Muslims are trying to impose sharia law on America. They insist that Islam is a dangerous religion, as are immigrants from foreign countries with largely Muslim populations. For example, Act! for America, considered an anti-Muslim hate group by the Center for American Progress and the Southern Poverty Law Center, has one thousand chapters and actively promotes the idea that the government should not allow practicing Muslims to be US citizens. "A practicing Muslim who believes the word of the Koran to be the word of Allah . . . who goes to mosque and prays every Friday, who prays five times a day—this practicing Muslim, who believes in the teachings of the Koran, cannot be a loyal citizen of the United States,"[10] states Brigitte Gabriel, president of Act! for America.

> "I am afraid that on the train home from the hospital, someone will think my backpack contains a bomb."[11]
>
> —Mubeen Shakir, medical student

The impacts of the words and actions of these groups can be felt by Muslim Americans just going about their everyday tasks. Whenever he is in public, Mubeen Shakir, a Muslim American who was born in the United States, worries about what might happen. He is a Rhodes scholar, a student at Harvard Medical School, and has many American friends who are not Muslim. However, for now, he lives with the fear that others affected by Islamophobia will hurt him or his family. "I am afraid that on the train home from the hospital, someone will think my backpack contains a bomb," Shakir writes. "When I walk through a crowd, I fear being accosted by young men calling me 'Arab' or 'terrorist.' I am afraid that all the talk of Muslim registries, rabid dogs and closing mosques will lead to someone shooting at the mosque my mother attends everyday."[11]

Fear Leads to Discrimination

Even if most citizens did not condone hate crimes or hostility toward Muslim Americans, unjust fears often lead to discrimination. CAIR published data that showed bias incidents in California against Muslims increased by 58 percent from 2014 to 2015 following the San Bernardino shooting. While reports of hate crimes were common in these bias incident reports, Muslim Americans also filed complaints involving employment and housing discrimination, school bullying, and unjustified or excessive interactions with law enforcement.

Sometimes the prejudice is unspoken, but in other cases it is vocal. In 2016 Rasheed Albeshari and his friends were playing volleyball by Lake Chabot in Northern California and took a break to pray. While they were praying, Albeshari heard a woman start screaming at them. He turned his camera on and recorded Denise Slader, who shouted, "You are very deceived by Satan. Your mind has been taken over, brainwashed."[12] For Albeshari and other Muslim Americans, dealing with

Samantha Elauf, right, and her mother, Majda Elauf, stand outside the US Supreme Court building where the justices were considering her case against Abercrombie & Fitch. The retailer did not hire her because her hijab conflicted with the company's dress code. The justices ultimately ruled in her favor.

harassment like this has become commonplace, especially after any type of violent event to which Muslims are connected.

The workplace is another area in which Muslims are affected by Islamophobia. Muslim American women and men have found that if anything indicates to others that they are Muslim, from their clothing to asking for a space to pray, it can result in negativity from coworkers and bosses. For example, Muslim women have experienced criticism for wearing a hijab at work. In June 2015 the US Supreme Court ruled in favor of Samantha Elauf, who applied for a job at Abercrombie & Fitch but was denied a position because her hijab was, according to the company, not in line with the company's dress code. Despite a victory against the company, Muslim women still report discrimination due to their hijab at work. In 2020 Stefanae Coleman went to work at Chicken Express, a fast food restaurant. "I converted to Islam not too long ago and I started wearing my hijab, I went to work today and was kicked out because my hijab was not [a part of] the 'dress code' apparently and I wasn't allowed to wear it,"[13] she posted on social media. Later, Chicken Express apologized, but incidents like this still occur across the United States.

Dealing with It

Whether at work or out socially, Muslim Americans have to deal with the immediate and lingering effects of Islamophobia. Some choose to keep their religion private. They do not pray in public, do not wear any clothing associated with Islam, and attempt to blend in to avoid confrontation. Others face discrimination by speaking out against it. Still others continue living as a Muslim and hope that others learn to accept their religion. "I practice a sort of deliberate casualness about my Islam," explains Fatima Elkabti, a Muslim American living in Tyler, Texas. "My son attends Spanish immersion and Islamic day cares. I do not hide that I'm fasting in Ramadan but don't make much ado of it either. I want being Muslim American, at least among my friends out here, to be a variation of normal."[14]

CHAPTER TWO

Growing Up Muslim

Approximately 1.3 million Muslim Americans are under age eighteen. They are like any other young people in America—they go to school, spend time with friends, and interact with family. They are forging identities and discovering how they fit into society. However, for most of these young people, growing up in the United States means encountering discrimination in all areas of their lives. In schools, at jobs, and at social gatherings, young Muslim Americans face bias—and they learn to deal with it in different ways.

School Issues

Most young people do not face discrimination as very young children because they spend most of their time with their family and friends. It is when they go to school that Muslim American youth normally first encounter being stereotyped, insulted, and bullied. In a 2017 survey about bullying in relation to religious beliefs, the Institute for Social Policy and Understanding found that 42 percent of Muslims with children in K–12 schools said their children had been bullied for their religious beliefs. Also in 2017, a California chapter of CAIR conducted a survey of 1,041 students and found that more than half of Muslim students in the survey said they had been mocked, verbally insulted, or abused because of their religion.

In some of these types of cases, violence has occurred. In 2019 at East Brunswick High School in New Jersey, a Snapchat video captured by a student showed a female Muslim American student lying on the floor and being punched by another girl. The attacker also allegedly insulted the Muslim student with a verbal slur in a Snapchat video. The East Brunswick Public Schools superintendent, Victor Valeski, reported in a letter sent out to the school community that as the fight escalated, the aggressor pulled off the other girl's hijab and started screaming anti-Muslim slurs at her. The former was arrested and charged with simple assault, harassment, cyber harassment, and disorderly conduct, according to Middlesex County prosecutors. Because the school has a zero-tolerance policy for fighting, the Muslim American student was suspended for being involved in a fight. At a school board meeting after the attack, hundreds of students and parents showed up to protest the suspension. The Muslim American boy who filmed the video was also suspended for violating a school policy that prohibits students from posting unauthor-

Two students work together on a science project. Muslim young people, like young people everywhere, are forging their identities through the interactions they have at school, at home, and in many other settings.

ized photographs of classmates and staff. After the school board meeting, the board and Valeski announced they would review the zero-tolerance policy in the future, realizing that it was unfair to punish a student under attack.

Other Muslim students also endure less violent but still hurtful incidents at school. The words of fellow students hurt them, and often they are not sure how to respond. "This girl told me I was going to hell because I'm Muslim," says high school senior Sara Shohoud about her first incident of Islamophobia, when she was in first grade. "I didn't know how to counter it. I was so young. And now, I just keep quiet."[15]

> "This girl told me I was going to hell because I'm Muslim."[15]
>
> —Sara Shohoud, high school senior

Often the bullying is repeated, and when one student initiates it, others seem to follow. One day, while driving his son home from school, Mansoor Shams, a US marine, says his child opened up about the torments he received because of his faith. His child had accumulated a list of names and insults he had endured from other students. The list included slurs such as "terrorist," "Taliban," "Osama bin Laden," "bomber," and "killer." Shams's son spoke of being targeted in other hateful incidents. "A child approached my son's open classroom door and yelled 'Allahu Akbar (God is great) you're all going to die,' slammed the door shut and ran off down the hallway,"[16] Shams writes. For young Muslims, these incidents can make school scary and uncomfortable.

> "A child approached my son's open classroom door and yelled 'Allahu Akbar (God is great) you're all going to die,' slammed the door shut and ran off down the hallway."[16]
>
> —Mansoor Shams, a US marine

Not Just Students

What is more difficult is that Muslim Americans cannot always depend on teachers to stand up for them. Some teachers are even the perpetrators of bias toward Muslim students. In some cases, the teachers may not intend to make the students uncomfortable, but the stereotypes in their comments still cause

Schools Add Muslim Holidays to Their Calendars

One method that schools are adopting to help end cultural bias against Muslims is to include the Muslim holidays in their school calendar. In 2015 New York City mayor Bill de Blasio announced that New York would close public schools for the two most important Muslim holidays. Municipalities across the country also include in their school calendars the two holy days, Eid al-Adha, known as the Festival of Sacrifice (in honor of Abraham's willingness to sacrifice his son to God); and Eid al-Fitr, which signifies the end of Ramadan, the holy month of fasting. But New York City is the largest of these cities, with over 1 million school children. These holidays are included in addition to religious holidays already on the calendar—such as the Jewish holiday Rosh Hashanah and the Christian holiday Christmas. Helal Chowdhury, a sophomore at Brooklyn Technical High School, says that he used to have to decide between going to school and not getting behind or celebrating a holiday with his family. "This is a big step forward," the fifteen-year-old says. "We've been waiting a long time for this."

Quoted in Michael Grynbaum and Sharon Otterman, "New York City Adds 2 Muslim Holy Days to Public School Calendar," *New York Times*, March 5, 2015. www.nytimes.com.

discomfort. In 2016 Sumaya Ali, a tenth grader, attended her world history class at Leuzinger High School in Lawndale, California. While in class, she said that a teacher asked his students if any of them thought all Muslims should die. The teacher was lecturing about Republican presidential candidate Donald Trump and his view on Muslims. After the question, a few students raised their hands. Another time, after a student informed the teacher that Ali was Muslim, Ali says that the teacher said to her, "Oh, you're a terrorist," and then added, "That's not what I think. That's what America thinks."[17] Ali felt extremely uncomfortable after these discussions, and eventually administrators switched her to another class after her brother let them know about the comments. However, the teacher was not reprimanded.

In another incident, a younger student was allegedly called a terrorist by his teacher. In Fort Bend, Texas, twelve-year-old Waleed Abushaaban was watching a movie with his class when his teacher made a comment to him about terrorism. He did not know if the comment had anything to do with the movie, *Bend It like Beckham*, which features a young woman of Indian descent. However, in the movie the character is a Sikh, not a Muslim. "We're in the class watching a movie," explains Abushaaban, "and I was just laughing at the movie and the teacher said, 'I

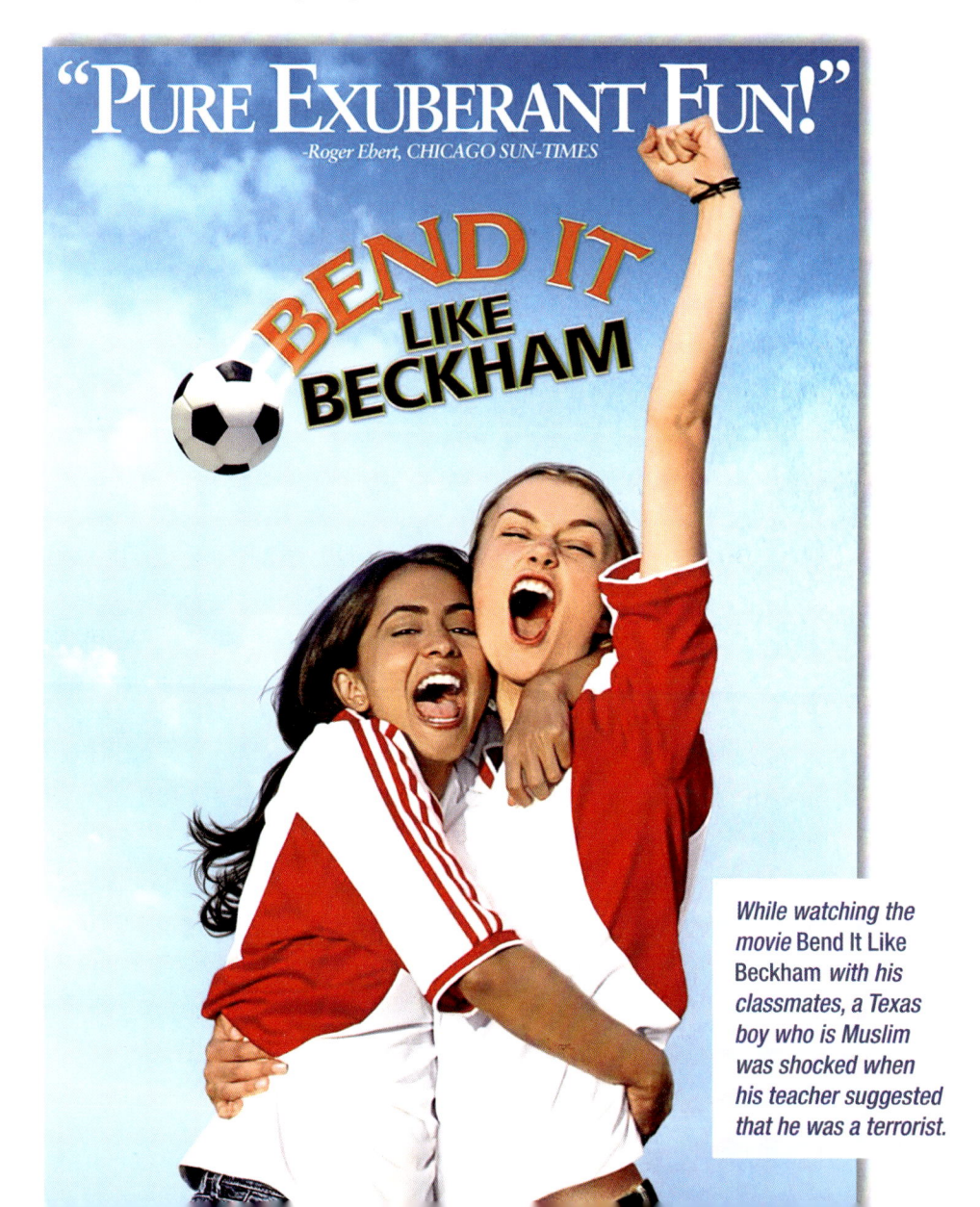

While watching the movie Bend It Like Beckham *with his classmates, a Texas boy who is Muslim was shocked when his teacher suggested that he was a terrorist.*

wouldn't be laughing if I was you.' And I said why? She said, 'because we all think you're a terrorist.'"[18] After that comment, other kids started laughing at him and making jokes about him being a terrorist and carrying a bomb. School officials placed the teacher on administrative leave. During an investigation the teacher said she was just pointing out negative stereotypes. However, school officials, said her comments were inappropriate.

Preventing Bias in Education

School districts have a legal obligation to protect their students from bullying, and many are attempting to do that and more. Some schools are taking a proactive approach to ensure that incidents like these do not occur in the future. In 2017 the Oakland County, Michigan, school system offered cultural training to teachers about tolerance and respect. Huda Essa, a Michigan woman, Muslim, and former teacher, led the training. Teachers and other staff attended a mandatory three-hour presentation by Essa that focused on how to create a respectful environment for children of multicultural backgrounds.

The training was based on Essa's book, *Teach Us Your Name*, which gives teachers tips on how to respect and empower all children to take pride in their heritage. "It really was about creating a respectful environment for all students,"[19] says Steve Matthews, superintendent of the Novi Community School District. Despite the fact that the school system believes there is value in this program, there has been backlash by community Christian groups that claim Essa's training has an anti-Christian agenda. Essa and the school district counter that the training was about inclusiveness and say there were no offensive comments about Christianity or other faiths in it.

The federal government has also provided guidance on how to prevent bullying based on any type of discrimination in schools. The US Department of Education (DOE) website recommends, specifically for working against Muslim bias, that schools incorporate the experiences, perspectives, and words of Muslim peo-

The Clock Scare

When he was in high school, Ahmed Mohamed's goal was to go to the Massachusetts Institute of Technology, so he spent his free time studying and working with technology. He never imagined his love of science would land him in handcuffs. In 2015 his homemade alarm clock got him suspended from his suburban Irving, Texas, high school. He had brought the reassembled digital clock to show his teachers his accomplishment. His English teacher thought the clock resembled a bomb and sent Mohamed to the administration. Police officers were summoned, and Mohamed was handcuffed and taken into custody, accused of intentionally perpetrating a bomb scare. The police investigated, decided there was no malicious intent, and did not charge Mohamed. Mohamed, his family, and many supporters believe he was unjustly accused because of his Sudanese ancestry and Muslim faith. Then-president Barack Obama as well as other politicians praised Mohamed for his technical ability, and he was invited to participate in science and technology events held by Google and other industry leaders. His family, however, continued to receive threats and attacks from people who believed unfounded claims that he and his family were terrorists. Eventually, his parents withdrew him and his siblings from their schools in the Irving Independent School District and moved to Qatar.

ple into their curriculum for areas such as social studies, current events, and literature. It also suggests that teachers include Islam and its history and beliefs in discussions of world religions. The department's recommendation also stresses teaching students to recognize biased words and actions and to be an ally to others against bullying. Jinnie Spiegler, director of curriculum at the Anti-Defamation League, and Sarah Sisaye of the Office of Safe and Healthy Students at the Department of Education write, "Educators play a vital role in fostering safe, welcoming learning communities for their students, and, given the unsettling rise in anti-Muslim prejudice, the efforts teachers make to support all of their students and build understanding and respect are more critical than ever."[20]

Encountering Prejudice Outside of School

Muslim American youth also encounter bias outside of school. In 2016 Yaasameen Al-Hamdani researched and produced a study, "Islamophobia and the Young American Experience," for her master's degree thesis at Middle Tennessee State University. She interviewed six focus groups with a total of twenty-six participants who self-identify as Muslim American. She asked questions regarding experiences growing up in America as a Muslim. Many said that when going out in public, some people would make negative comments to them. One participant said, "My mom and I have been followed in Costco by a man throughout the store. He was coming up behind us and saying mean things like, 'What are you doing here? Go back to your country.'"[21]

Incidents and preconceptions like these cause young Muslims to worry about even engaging in routine activities. Some Muslim Americans find stress in just wanting to practice the traditions of their religion. For example, many practicing Muslims pray five times a day, and being out and about when it is time to pray

A young Muslim boy takes the traditional pose for prayer. American Muslims who follow their faith's prayer traditions worry about how other people will react.

causes some Muslim Americans anxiety. They worry about others' reactions if they bring out their prayer mats to kneel on. When in high school, Hana Alasry took a class at a community college and found herself on campus during two of the five times a day she was to pray. While she did not encounter any criticism for her praying, she often was anxious about how others would react. "In several instances, I found myself praying in an empty hallway only to begin sweating out of fear when someone unexpectedly walked by," Alasry recalls. "In fact, in full honesty, sometimes I would place my red folder on the floor and if someone passed by, I would pick it up as if to retrieve a paper from inside."[22] Her fear came from the bias she has seen against Muslim Americans.

Another common experience is simply being singled out as different. Many young Muslim Americans deal with comments that might not be intended as insults but make them feel separate from other Americans. Because of their appearance, whether due to clothing or ethnicity, some non-Muslim Americans assume that Muslim Americans are not "true" Americans. A participant in Al-Hamdani's study recalled this happening when he tried to get his driver's license in Alabama, stating, "The man that worked at the DMV said, 'You need to go to Birmingham because we don't process internationals in Jacksonville,' even after I told him I was an American."[23] Comments like that tend to leave youth feeling that they are different and separate from Americans as a whole.

Daily Stress

Dealing with these negative experiences on a daily basis leaves many young Muslim Americans stressed. They struggle to understand what is happening to them and their communities, to figure out how to respond to bias or outright hate, and to manage fear. Hebh Jamal grew up in the Bronx borough of New York City, and while she felt insulated from Islamophobia earlier in life, during her teen years she dealt with the challenges of being a Muslim in America. She recounts facing anti-Muslim sentiment regularly, and she often worried about how and why society

> "Experiencing stressful events earlier on in the life course—school age—has significant and lasting effects on health and well-being over a child's life span."[25]
>
> —Sirry Alang, assistant professor of sociology at Lehigh University

perceived her differently. She felt like she had to constantly defend being Muslim and put in effort to teach people the difference between herself and terrorists who commit violent acts in the name of Islam. "You feel like the whole world is against you," Jamal says. "It's exhausting."[24]

The type of daily stress that Muslim American youth deal with has both physical and psychological impacts. Sirry Alang, an assistant professor in the Department of Sociology at Lehigh University in Bethlehem, Pennsylvania, says:

> Experiencing stressful events earlier on in the life course—school age—has significant and lasting effects on health and well-being over a child's life span. Things like psychological distress, emotional and behavioral problems, poor academic performances. It also increases risks of physiological and chronic conditions that are linked to stress, like gastrointestinal issues, cardiovascular diseases, that not only affect the child but tax other systems such as healthcare, education, and social services.[25]

Thus, fear, repressed anger, and concerns over social acceptance can impair the health of young Muslim Americans and negatively affect how they see the world around them.

How They Cope

Muslim American youth have developed different coping mechanisms to deal with bias, discrimination, and bullying in order to mitigate the stress in their lives. Some choose to hide or downplay their Muslim identity to avoid confrontation. Nineteen-year-old Zayneb Almiggabber, who was born and raised in the New York area, downplayed her ethnic identity as a kid because many considered her Arab heritage synonymous with being a Muslim. "I guess I didn't tell a lot of people I was Arab in high school, now that I think about it," says Almiggabber, whose father is from Egypt and whose mother is from New York. "I'd tell people I was Mediterranean and they'd guess Italian or Greek and I wouldn't correct them."[26] But as she got older, she embraced her ethnic and Muslim heritages and now speaks openly about those facets of her identity.

To help Muslim American youth like Almiggabber embrace their identity and cope with potential discrimination, a few organizations have come to their aid. One such ally is the Youth Speakers Training program. Launched in 2016, Youth Speakers Training is a community service to help school-aged Muslim Americans learn how to deal with bullying. It also helps them learn more about their faith and share this with others. They discover how to work with others to make their school environment more inclusive. This program is offered in California and seven other states by the nonprofit Islamic Networks Group. During a session in San Jose, California, Muslim American students discussed their rights at school and brainstormed how to respond to difficult scenarios, such as what to do if another student jokes about the Muslim student bombing the school. They discussed turning the questions back onto the person who asked so that those individuals have to confront their own biases. Ishaq Pathan, a director of the program in the Bay Area, believes this is a good strategy to build dialogue instead of dismissing the ignorance or simply resenting those who often unknowingly accept pervasive stereotypes. "None of this works if we just turn around and make fun of other people," says Pathan. "It's only going to work if we all reduce this thing together."[27]

Ultimately, programs like Youth Speakers Training help Muslim American youth feel comfortable with who they are—Americans who practice the Islamic faith. This combined with efforts in schools to combat cultural bias is the hope for the future. According to Nadia Ansary, an associate professor at Rider University in New Jersey who studies discrimination and bullying of Muslim youth, "Everybody has a right to be educated in an environment where they're not abused. Everybody has a right to practice their faith traditions."[28]

CHAPTER THREE

Hate Crimes

Many Muslim Americans contend with discrimination in their daily lives. Misinformation and misconceptions about terrorists, lack of familiarity with Islam and its traditions, and the human desire to find scapegoats for larger social problems make it difficult to unseat that bias. Occasionally, though, more hostile forms of prejudice arise. Unreasoned anger and fear of others can result in violence and hate-motivated crimes. Hate crimes are those in which perpetrators act on the basis of a bias against the victim's race, color, religion, or national origin. Such crimes have been committed against Muslim Americans, and they create fear in Muslim communities as well as aggravate social tensions.

Fear and Hate in Minneapolis

Muslim Americans living in Minneapolis, Minnesota, were particularly fearful in 2015 and 2016 when violent incidents against them flared in the city and its surroundings. The 2016 election approached, and political rhetoric against Muslims increased after the 2015 San Bernardino shooting, a terrorist attack by an extremist Muslim couple. The large immigrant Somali Muslim population in Minneapolis witnessed a high number of hate crimes in this time period. For one, on October 30, 2015, Asma Jama, a Muslim woman of Somali descent and Kenyan nationality, spoke Swahili at an Applebee's restaurant and was attacked by a white patron who demanded that Jama speak English. The perpetrator was charged with assault. In June 2016 a Muslim halal shop, a deli that prepares meat in accordance with Muslim law, was vandalized. But the most violent incident occurred on June 29, 2016, when a man named Anthony Sawina shot at five Somali Americans who were on their way to morning prayer in Minneapolis.

It was 2:30 a.m., and the five Muslim American men were walking to their car after playing basketball. From there they planned to go to the mosque for prayers. Before reaching the car, they encountered Sawina and a group of people with him, who were emerging from a bar. The five Muslim American men, including one who was wearing a traditional Muslim prayer robe, ignored the insults yelled at them by Sawina and the others, and

Asma Jama (left) was speaking Swahili at a restaurant when she was attacked by a white patron who demanded she speak English. Here she joins others who are calling for stricter penalties for felony assaults motivated by bias.

started to get in the car. But then one of the Muslim men objected to something that one of Sawina's group yelled at them. Sawina had a gun. He aimed it at the car's windshield but did not fire. Next he headed toward the back of the car. He fired at least two shots through an open door. Two men sitting in the back seat were shot in the legs and another bullet just missed the driver's head. After the shooting Sawina ran away. A witness later identified Sawina to the police as the shooter and he was arrested about a month later.

Sawina was charged with five counts of second-degree assault in connection with the case. In court he claimed that he was defending himself, despite the fact that none of the five Muslim men had a weapon. A district court jury rejected Sawina's self-defense argument and found him guilty of nine counts of assault and attempted first- and second-degree murder. The judge sentenced Sawina to thirty-nine years in jail, explaining that the punishment was tied to the fact that the crime was racially motivated and that Sawina endangered others by firing in a public place. And while the Muslim community was relieved to see Sawina and the other perpetrators prosecuted, it did not take away the fear that they would be targeted again.

FBI Findings

Muslim American fears are supported by statistics from those times. According to the *American Journal of Public Health*, hate crimes against Muslims in the United States in 2016 were five times more common than before September 11, 2001. Similarly, the Pew Research Center found that the total number of anti-Muslim incidents had risen 67 percent, from 154 in 2014 to 257 in 2015. The following year there were 307 incidents of anti-Muslim hate crimes, which was a 19 percent increase from the previous year.

Hate crimes against Muslim Americans tend to be cyclical. These types of crimes increase after incidents involving Islamist extremists and when politicians engage in anti-Muslim rhetoric. They decrease in years that have not experienced incidents in-

Deepening the Muslim-Jewish Bond

Those of Muslim and Jewish faiths are not typically thought of as allies, largely because of a history of conflicts in the Middle East between Israel and its Arab neighbors. But since both groups have dealt with hate crimes in the United States and around the world, they have developed a bond. In many cases, they fight together against discrimination and help each other cope with tragic events. For example, Muslim groups helped raise hundreds of thousands of dollars to help Pittsburgh's Tree of Life Synagogue recover after a gunman killed eleven people there in 2018. The Jewish congregation at the synagogue then had a fundraiser for New Zealand's Muslims after a white supremacist shooter killed fifty-one people at two mosques in 2019. Different organizations that include these two groups have formed. The Muslim-Jewish Advisory Council was established by the American Jewish Committee and the Islamic Society of North America to work for legislation to improve the tracking of hate crimes. Other partnerships have developed as people find common ground on the unifying issue of preventing hate crimes.

volving Islamist extremists. For example, in 2018 the FBI reported that Muslim American hate crimes had decreased to 270. In that year there were no major Islamist-related incidents in the United States. New America, a nonpartisan, nonprofit think tank, developed a new data visualization project that tracks trends in anti-Muslim activities at the state and local level in the United States since 2012. Its graphs show that while anti-Muslim incidents rise after terrorist attacks, they also occur after politicians make derogatory or controversial comments about Muslim Americans. Robert McKenzie, a senior fellow at New America and director of this project, points to several of the controversial comments made by Donald Trump and insists that the evidence reveals that "political rhetoric from national leaders has a real and measurable impact."[29] The project continues to update as new data come in to see whether the trends continue.

Targeting Mosques and Islamic Centers

Hate crimes range from graffiti on a mosque to murder. All are meant to incite fear in a group. A common hate crime toward Muslims is damaging a Muslim gathering place such as a mosque or Islamic center. In 2017 more than one hundred mosques in the United States were targeted with arson, threats, and vandalism, according to CAIR.

One of these mosques was in Bloomington, Minnesota. In 2018 the US Department of Justice charged Michael McWhorter, Joe Morris, and Michael Hari with using an explosive device to damage Bloomington's Dar Al-Farooq Islamic Center. The bombing had occurred the previous year. The men had traveled from Illinois to Minnesota, leaving their cell phones at home and avoiding toll roads to avoid being electronically tracked, to specifically carry out the attack on the mosque. They threw a pipe bomb into the office of the imam, or Islamic religious leader, and smashed the windows of the mosque. Because the attack took place before morning prayers, no one was injured. When authorities arrested the three men, McWhorter told federal agents that he and the others "did not intend to kill anyone but wanted to 'scare them out of the country' because they [Muslims] push their beliefs on everyone else."[30] The men were part of a militia group that intended to oust Muslims from the United States.

Several other militia group members also have plotted to harm Muslim Americans. In 2019 a federal jury in Kansas convicted Curtis Allen, Gavin Wright, and Patrick Eugene Stein of a bombing plot against Muslim Americans. These men, who belonged to a militia called the Crusaders, planned to bomb Somali immigrants at a mosque and an apartment complex in Wichita right after the November 2016 US elections. They intended to detonate four vehicles packed with explosives at the corners of the apartment complex. However, they were arrested

> "[A hate crime] creates fear all over the world. People watch incidents like this and think it could happen to them. It has a rippling effect."[31]
>
> —John Rainey, US District Judge

about a month before Election Day when an informant notified the FBI. At sentencing, each man received from twenty-five to thirty years in federal prison.

In another event, an individual committed arson against a mosque and Islamic community center in Victoria, Texas. Marq Vincent Perez was found guilty in 2018 of the use of fire to commit a felony, the possession of an unregistered destructive device, and a hate crime. He was sentenced to twenty-six years in federal prison. US District Judge John Rainey explains how such crimes are like a cancer that must be stopped: "It creates fear all over the world," Rainey says. "People watch incidents like this and think it could happen to them. It has a rippling effect."[31]

The Islamic Center of Victoria, a mosque located in Texas, burns. The center's destruction sparked fear and anxiety in the city's Muslim community.

Muslim Americans worry about this rippling effect, and they live with fear that such incidents will happen again. Thus, they must worry about their safety when doing something as normal as attending a mosque to pray, holding services, or attending events together. Dr. Shahid Hashmi, president of the Victoria Islamic Center and a local surgeon, says that since the Texas mosque's destruction, the Muslim community is scared to live normally. He explains that some female members have stopped wearing head coverings in public, while others will not pray at the new mosque that was built. "The peace has been shattered,"[32] Hashmi says.

Personal Attacks

Mosques are not the only targets of anti-Muslim hate crimes. In 2016 James Benjamin Jones threatened the owners of two grocery

Hate Crime or Freedom of Speech?

While yelling a hateful name at a Muslim American is an example of bias, it is not a crime. Hateful speech is still protected as free speech, which gives people the right to call others' names if they desire. By law, for hate speech to be considered a crime, it must directly incite imminent criminal activity or threaten violence against a specific group or individual. When such occurs, the person can be charged with a hate crime. However, some feel that hate speech itself should be designated as a crime. Richard Stengel, a former official in the Barack Obama administration, writes, "All speech is not equal. And where truth cannot drive out lies, we must add new guardrails." He specifically cites hateful speech toward Muslims as speech that should not be protected. Many, however, fear that such a hate speech law is a step toward eroding the First Amendment of the Constitution, which protects people's right to speak their minds, however unpopular their views may be. The fear is that once one form of free expression is made illegal, another will follow; from this viewpoint, in order to preserve Americans' free expression right, hate speech should be allowed.

Richard Stengel, "Why America Needs a Hate Speech Law," *Washington Post*, October 29, 2019. www.washingtonpost.com.

stores in Fort Myers in southwest Florida. Southwest Florida is home to a small population of Muslims, some of whom are American-born and others who have come from the Middle East, Southeast Asia, or Europe. Both stores visited by Jones sell halal meats to Muslims who live in the area. During a court hearing, Jones admitted to threatening violence against the owner of the Halal Meat and Grocery Store if he did not permanently close the store. That threat was made in June. Then in July, according to court testimony, Jones issued a similar threat against the owner of the Sahara Mediterranean Market. Jones also threatened the business owner's family, warning that they all might come to harm if the family did not leave the area. In February 2017 Jones pleaded guilty to two federal hate crimes for his threats against the two Muslim grocery stores.

Other hate crimes move beyond threats to personal attacks. And the mocking and physical harm to Muslim Americans even comes at the hands of young people. In 2019 twelve-year-old Julius Lara and fourteen-year-old Syend Smith allegedly began punching Muslim American school safety agent Md Islam, who was on his way to his car after leaving a bank in the Bronx in New York City. The youths approached him, taunted him, and then started hitting him when he refused to respond to their jeers. Islam was transported to the hospital and treated for pain to his neck and shoulders. Both youngsters were arrested. They were charged with intent to cause physical injury and a hate crime because their actions were allegedly motivated by religious bias.

As with Md Islam, other Muslim victims are typically just going about their business when assaulted. In 2020 a young Muslim woman, a foreign exchange student from Saudi Arabia, was standing in a Portland, Oregon, train station. Another woman, Jasmine Renee Campbell, allegedly tore off the victim's hijab and tried to choke her with it. Campbell also allegedly mocked the victim's religion and made fun of her hijab. Campbell told police that she wanted the victim to know she did not have to be a Muslim. The prosecutor indicted Campbell for a hate crime of attempted strangulation, harassment, and criminal mischief. The episode scared the victim to the point that she now wears a hat to cover her head instead of a head scarf, fearing other attacks.

Muslim American Response

Dealing with the aftermath of attacks and the fear of future violence has prompted different reactions in Muslim communities. Some have decided that self-defense is the best method to reduce the chance of being targeted. Owning a gun is one means of self-protection that Muslim Americans have turned to. Hassan Shibly is the son of Syrian immigrants and the executive director of the CAIR chapter in Florida. He has been harassed and has even received death threats as a result of his work advocating for Muslim American rights. He bought a gun to protect himself. "I'm not a reckless gun enthusiast," says Shibly. "I'm somebody who reluctantly owns these tools for purposes of self-defense, while recognizing the great burden they come with."[33]

Other Muslim Americans believe that better protection and prevention can result from tougher legislation against hate crimes. For one, they call for hate crime laws in the four states that did not have them as of 2020—Arkansas, Georgia, South Carolina, and Wyoming. Also, they work with other religious advocacy groups to fight against white nationalism, an ideology that blames non-Christian faiths and nonwhite ethnicities for problems in the world. In 2019 the Muslim Advocates, the Union for Reform Judaism, the NAACP Legal Defense and Educational Fund, the Leadership Conference on Civil and Human Rights, and the Sikh Coalition, all nonprofit organizations, sent a letter to the FBI requesting to meet and discuss the continued threat of white nationalist violence to houses of worship and vulnerable communities. Muslim Advocates is also launching a petition campaign urging the FBI to focus on the threat of white nationalism. Other Muslim organizations are taking similar steps to raise awareness of the issue and fight for justice for those who are targeted because of their religion or race.

Community Response

Working together with communities has helped ease the hate crime burdens that many Muslim Americans carry. Communities have rallied around victims and stood in support of the fight against hate crimes. As an example, in 2017 Ashfaq Taufique, president of the Birmingham Islamic Society in Hoover, Alabama, reported a threatening email to the local police department. The email stated that all Muslims, along with Mexican and African Americans, would be hunted nationwide until dead and gone. The police took the threat seriously and provided extra patrols in the area. More than that, Taufique was surprised and touched by his community's outpouring of support. "With all the hate and fear-mongering going on, there has been an overwhelming number of supportive emails and mail, from all over the place," Taufique says. "People were showing up with cookies and flowers and cards. The community at large

Communities touched by anti-Muslim violence have come together as one. This happened in Victoria, Texas, and also in Bloomington, Minnesota. After an attack on the Dar Al-Farooq Islamic Center in Bloomington, the community rallied (pictured) in a show of support.

> "With all the hate and fear-mongering going on, there has been an overwhelming number of supportive emails and mail, from all over the place."[34]
>
> —Ashfaq Taufique, president of the Birmingham Islamic Society

has a desire to come and be with us."[34] In gratitude, the Hoover Crescent Islamic Center hosted an open house to welcome visitors who wanted to learn more about Islam and Muslim traditions.

Other communities have also seen positivity emerge in response to hate. After the burning of the mosque in Victoria, Texas, the Muslim community decided to rebuild. Soon, they found many people of all faiths throughout the Victoria community donating to the cause. The mosque fund received over $1 million in donations and used this to rebuild and reopen in 2018. During the rebuilding, members of B'nai Israel opened up their synagogue to the Muslim community as a place to worship, and four churches in the town also offered space for the mosque's Muslim congregation to hold services. Abe Ajrami, a member of the Victoria mosque, is thankful for the positivity in his hometown. "This is a beautiful city and we have wonderful neighbors,"[35] Ajrami says. This gives many in the Muslim community hope that with time and efforts by their community, the government, and non-Muslims, hates crimes and bias will ease, if not disappear, in America.

CHAPTER FOUR

Political Impacts

Prejudice is not confined to individuals; it is systemic. It has become part of the social order, even as many seek to identify it and remove it. Discrimination against Muslim Americans is no exception. Differences in faith, traditions, and appearance have set Muslims apart from mainstream American culture, and unfortunately, these differences become amplified when politicians and the government feed and perpetuate that bias. Whether politicians' actions and words are meant to incite bias or not, studies show that they do. Since they are public figures, government representatives are listened to by many people, and some take these representatives' words as a reason to treat Muslim Americans with disrespect.

The 9/11 tragedy was the defining event that caused suspicion and even bitterness toward Muslims, and Muslim Americans saw a major spike in bias-fueled incidents against them in the months afterward. Then, when President George W. Bush declared a war on terror, the US government called on other countries to fight terrorists and those supporting them. Bush's war played out domestically and globally. He initiated a war in Afghanistan to hunt al Qaeda and enacted domestic security measures meant to protect the country from all terrorists. During this time, Bush sought to assure all Americans that Muslims themselves were not the enemy and that instead the enemy was the Islamist extremists.

Despite Bush's assurances, many Muslim Americans felt that the war on terror's domestic policies targeted them. Specifically, the government put the Patriot Act into law to strengthen security. This act allowed for indefinite detention of immigrants, gave law enforcement permission to search a home or business without the owner's or occupant's consent or knowledge, and expanded the use of National Security Letters, which let the FBI search telephone, email, and financial records without a court order. Muslim Americans feel that people in their communities were unjustly targeted by these actions. They believe that Muslim Americans were unfairly profiled and had their homes and records searched without any basis aside from their religion. After ten years of the Patriot Act, Farhana Khera, executive director of Muslim Advocates, wrote, "During the last decade, Muslim Advocates has found the FBI has increasingly focused its powers on law-abiding citizens, not based on criminal behavior, but based on race, ethnicity and religious or political beliefs."[36]

A US soldier searches a villager in southeastern Afghanistan in 2002. The war on terror, which began in Afghanistan but also resulted in new domestic policies, left many American Muslims feeling like they were the targets of those policies.

Partisan Divide

In the United States political parties are divided on how they view Muslim Americans. Most of the government officials who use anti-Muslim rhetoric and support legislation that seems to target Muslim Americans are Republicans. As president of the United States, Donald Trump leads the Republican Party, so many of these conservatives, from other politicians to constituents, are influenced by his negative tweets or words about Islam and his proposals such as the Muslim ban. New America, a think tank working with the American Muslim Institution, conducted 1,165 interviews in four metropolitan areas prior to the November 2018 midterm elections and found that 60 percent of Republicans agreed with the idea that Muslim Americans were not as patriotic as non-Muslim Americans, compared to 38 percent of the public overall. Additionally, 56 percent of Republicans surveyed agreed that they would be concerned if a mosque or Islamic center were constructed in their neighborhood, compared to an overall level of 33 percent. While not all Republicans share these views, these studies show that how people view Muslims is partly affected by what party they are affiliated with at the time.

Recent Times

Although hate crimes and assaults against Muslim Americans rose immediately following 9/11 and the institution of the Patriot Act, after a few years they started to decrease. However, in 2015, following the San Bernardino shooting, some in the political world responded with words and proposed actions that specifically targeted Muslims. In 2016, during his presidential campaign, Donald Trump said, "I think Islam hates us."[37] Around the same time, he promised that if elected he would block immigration to the United States from predominately Muslim countries, what he referred to as a "Muslim ban." By not choosing his words more carefully, Trump's rhetoric cast a wide net that could suggest suspicion of Muslim Americans.

> "I think Islam hates us."[37]
>
> —Donald Trump, during the 2016 presidential campaign

That year hate crimes and bias incidents against Muslim American sharply rose. Research supports the connection between US politicians' words and actions and an increased fear of Muslim Americans. Trump repeated his call for a Muslim ban at several rallies, eliciting cheers, and made remarks about how, if he could implement action in 2015, he would consider closing all mosques in the United States. Other politicians followed suit, making similar statements, and Muslim Americans felt the effects. A 2016 report from the California State University, San Bernardino, Center for the Study of Hate and Extremism correlated insensitive or inflammatory political statements about Muslims with dates of crimes against Muslims. The study suggests that such political rhetoric is linked to rising hate crimes. The report states that anti-Muslim hate crimes in the United States increased in 2015 to the highest levels since just after the September 11, 2001, terror attacks. The report found that "a tolerant statement about Muslims by a political leader was accompanied by a sharp decline in hate crime, while a less tolerant announcement was followed by a precipitous increase in both the severity and number of anti-Muslim hate crimes."[38] It states that there was an increase of 87.5 percent in anti-Muslim hate crime in the days directly following Trump's 2015 announcement that he supported a total ban of Muslims entering the country for a period of time.

For Muslim Americans, Trump's words resulted in fear, and they were disappointed that many Americans seemed to agree with him. Aziz Ansari is a Muslim American actor, writer, producer, director, and comedian. He was born in California to parents who emigrated from India and are Muslim. In 2016 he felt it necessary to warn his mother not to pray at her mosque but to pray at home instead. As an American citizen, he felt sad that he should have to worry about how his mother worshipped, but he believed that Trump's words were xenophobic and increased anger and bias toward all Muslims. He felt she could be in danger. "Today, with the presidential candidate Donald J. Trump and others like him spewing hate speech, prejudice is reaching new levels. It's

Candidate Donald Trump works the crowd at a 2016 campaign rally. Trump elicited cheers from his supporters when, at campaign rallies, he called for a ban on Muslims entering the country.

visceral, and scary, and it affects how people live, work and pray," writes Ansari. "It makes me afraid for my family. It also makes no sense."[39] Many other Muslim Americans shared his view, wondering why they, normal people going about their day-to-day lives, were targeted by national leaders.

Muslim Ban

Muslim Americans' fears worsened when Trump was elected because he set out to enact his campaign promises, including his proposed Muslim ban. In 2017 Trump signed an executive order that banned foreign nationals from seven predominantly Muslim countries from entering the country for 90 days. The order also suspended entry into the country of all Syrian refugees indefinitely and prohibited any other refugees from coming into the country for 120 days. Many Americans, Muslim and non-Muslim, immediately protested the ban, claiming it was discriminatory and endangered the welfare of those seeking US protection.

Aspects of the ban, and later versions of it, were immediately blocked by federal courts. Those courts found each iteration to be blatantly anti-Muslim, unconstitutional, and an abuse of the president's power. However, in 2018 the US Supreme Court issued a 5–4 decision that allowed the third iteration of the ban to remain in place permanently. As a result, the United States currently bans people from Iran, Libya, Somalia, Syria, and Yemen, which are Muslim-majority countries, from coming to the United States on most or all types of visas, even if they have spouses, children, parents, or other family members living in the United States.

The public's reaction to the ban has been mixed. In February 2017 a CNN poll found that 53 percent of Americans opposed it and 47 percent favored it. An NBC/*Wall Street Journal* poll taken the same month found 44 percent saying the ban was necessary and 45 percent saying it is not needed. These narrow margins reveal how divided the nation was.

A crowd gathers in front of the US Supreme Court to protest the 2018 decision upholding President Donald Trump's travel ban on several Muslim-majority countries.

Some of those who continue to support the travel ban believe that Muslims make the United States unsafe and are trying to recruit others to their cause. Jennifer Mayers, a blogger who says her life is focused on living as a Christian, is one who unreservedly favors the ban. "I support President Trump's ban on Muslims from entering this country. And you should too," Mayers writes. "This is NOT a race issue. This is an issue about protecting us from Arabs who wish to blow us up and recruit our citizens into their depraved sick world."[40]

For Muslim Americans, the ban appears to be an issue of ethnicity and religion, and targeting predominantly Muslim nations makes them feel as if they are not welcome in their country. Abrar Omeish, a young Libyan American woman who lives in Fairfax, Virginia, felt a knot in her stomach when she heard that the Supreme Court upheld the travel ban after she had campaigned against it for months. She was getting married, and many of her family in Libya were not allowed to enter the United States to attend the ceremony because of the ban. "It's like we have to live as second-class citizens. We're not allowed to access our families just because we happen to be from a certain background, because we're Muslim,"[41] she says.

> "It's like we have to live as second-class citizens. We're not allowed to access our families just because we happen to be from a certain background, because we're Muslim."[41]
>
> —Abrar Omeish, American woman of Libyan descent

Like Omeish, many other Muslim Americans have family in other countries who are not allowed to enter the United States. Nearly all people who want to travel to the United States from the banned countries can only do so if they apply and are approved for a waiver. They must show that they would experience an undue hardship if they do not receive a visa, that they are not a threat to national security, and that their entry would be in the US national interest. According to the Brennan Center for Justice, an independent, nonpartisan law and policy organization, as of 2019 less than 30 percent of children of US citizens who applied

A Place for the Dead

In Worcester, Massachusetts, practicing Muslims just wanted a place to bury their dead. Therefore, in 2016 the Islamic Society of Greater Worcester sought approval to develop a Muslim cemetery on 55 acres (22.3 ha) of vacant farmland in Dudley, a town near Worcester. The Dudley Zoning Board, however, rejected the Islamic Society's application for a permit. The board stressed concerns that a cemetery could potentially contaminate groundwater and lower nearby property values, but the Islamic Society believed that anti-Muslim bias was part of the decision.

The Islamic Society filed a complaint in land court to overturn the decision, and federal prosecutors investigated whether the denial violated civil rights laws. The complaint and investigation were dropped in 2017 when an agreement was struck, allowing the Islamic Society to develop just 6 acres (2.4 ha) for burials. Yet some Dudley residents continued to protest the cemetery plan, citing water contamination, but others in the community felt that Islamophobia was the motivation.

The Islamic Society eventually decided to abandon plans to establish the cemetery in Dudley as expenses increased, and it instead worked toward an agreement with Worcester to reserve about fifteen hundred burial sites in a municipal cemetery. In April 2017 an agreement was reached, and Muslim residents now have a place for burial. "We had been struggling to get a Muslim burial for a long time and finally it has become a reality," says Khalid Sadozai, a member of the board of trustees at the Islamic Society. "We appreciate the help of the town for this."

Quoted in Cyrus Moulton, "After Controversy, a Muslim Burial at Hope Cemetery in Worcester," *Worcester (MA) Telegram*, October 28, 2017. www.telegram.com.

from these countries received waivers to come to their parent in the United States. Only 13 percent of spouses of US citizens received waivers.

Shaima Swileh, a Yemeni woman married to a US citizen, was in Yemen and applied for a waiver because her two-year-old son was dying in the United States. She was married to Ali Hassan, a US citizen who spent his youth in California after his family emigrated there from Yemen. In 2016 he and his family visited Yemen, where he met, fell in love with, and married Swileh. While he was still in Yemen, they had a child, and the boy became ill. Then the family stayed in Cairo, Egypt, where Swileh tried to obtain a waiver to bypass the ban. Her son had a degenerative brain condition, and she hoped he could receive medical treatment in the United States. She was repeatedly denied travel documents. Hassan went ahead, with their son, to America to get treatment. Her son, Abdullah, was admitted to UCSF Benioff Children's Hospital in Oakland, California. Swileh was denied entry until media and congressional pressure resulted in a waiver. Without their influence, she likely would not have been allowed in or been able to see her son just days before he died.

Opening the Door to More

Some observers believe the Muslim ban and Trump's words seem to have given other politicians the green light to make similar statements and take actions that target Muslims. Some politicians have included anti-Muslim views in speeches, social media posts, and announcements that reach the public. Muslim Americans also point to proposed legislative actions that target them, their communities, and places of worship. The politicians' words and actions, Muslim Americans believe, further incite negative views.

Social media has allowed politicians to share their views with many people at once. In 2018 Arkansas state senator Jason Rapert shared a Facebook article that stated that 95 percent of eligible Muslim Americans voted in the recent elections. He captioned his post asking if people wanted Muslims running America. In another tweet, Rapert stated, "Islam is the only belief system I am aware of in the world that directs its adherents to kill anyone

> "Islam is the only belief system I am aware of in the world that directs its adherents to kill anyone who refuses to convert to Islam or submit to Sharia Law."[42]
>
> —Jason Rapert, Arkansas state senator

who refuses to convert to Islam or submit to Sharia Law. Who would want to elect someone who believes this?"[42]

Several other lawmakers have made comments and taken actions that reflect Rapert's views. A 2018 analysis from BuzzFeed News, an online news agency, found that Republican officials in forty-nine states had openly attacked Muslims with words and proposed legislation since 2015. An Oklahoma representative, for example, refused to meet with Muslim constituents unless they replied to a questionnaire asking if they beat their wives. A Nebraska state senator suggested Muslims wanting to enter the United States should be made to eat pork, which is forbidden to practicing Muslims by the Koran. In yet another example, a Rhode Island state senator wrote in an email that Muslims seek to murder and rape non-Muslims.

In addition to the hurt and fear these statements elicit, Muslim Americans also worry that lawmakers will incite Islamophobia to get public support for federal, state, or local government legislation targeting Muslims. In 2016 the county board of Culpeper County, Virginia, denied a request from the Islamic Center of Culpeper for a sewage permit in order to prevent a mosque from being built. The request for the permit was rejected by the board in a 4-3 vote. When the county supervisor announced the decision, a roomful of citizens cheered. Similarly, the Sterling Heights Planning Commission in Michigan unanimously rejected a proposal from the American Islamic Community Center to build a mosque in the community. One official said that it would not fit in with surrounding properties. The campaign against the mosque was publicized widely in the area, and several elected officials, including the mayor, along with some members of the public, supported the decision. It was not until a Muslim organization sued the Sterling Heights Planning Commission that the council agreed to grant permission to build.

But many resistant residents did not approve of the decision, and six of them officially took the case to court, hoping to stop the building of the mosque. Some took to the streets protesting the construction, insisting that they did not want to live near Muslims. Resident Mike Gretel said, "You don't know what's going on. You know, they're cutting people's heads off, they killed our soldiers and everything. . . . They scare me. They scare everybody."[43] Despite the appeals and protests, the court upheld the agreement, paving the way for the mosque.

Many Muslim Americans get tired and frustrated because they must continually confront the negative views and actions of fellow citizens and their official representatives. However, they continue to work for tolerance because they believe the United States is their country too. The steps forward, such as the justice system allowing the building of the mosque, gives some hope. Azzam Elder, the lead lawyer for the American Islamic Community Center, says that he and the group "feel very relieved, because the city of Sterling Heights finally realized who they are: They're veterans who have served in the U.S. military; they're professionals; they're everyday Americans."[44]

CHAPTER FIVE

Finding Their Place

Despite the bias and discrimination that Muslim Americans have encountered, these citizens continue to push for acceptance and equality. Whether they were born in the United States or arrived as immigrants, Muslims want others to know their religion has no bearing on their status as Americans. They struggle to claim their rightful place in the cultural mix that defines the United States. As they do so, Muslim Americans are breaking new ground—becoming national sports figures, entertainers, and representatives in government—in their quest to live free of discrimination.

A Voice in the Government

Trump's travel ban spurred many Muslims to act by seeking office in hopes of adding their voices to more culturally sensitive legislation. Muslims are finding their ways into politics—from local to federal levels—and becoming civically involved in other ways. Since 2016 more than three hundred Muslim candidates, including more than one hundred women, have run for elected office nationwide, according to a report by CAIR. Because of their concern for their nation and its people, they are getting voted in. Once in office, they hope their example of working for all citizens will help decrease bias in others.

In 2020 the city of Cambridge, Massachusetts, elected Sumbul Siddiqui as mayor. Siddiqui immigrated to the United States from Pakistan when she was two. She graduated with a bachelor's degree in public policy from Brown University, served as an AmeriCorps fellow, and obtained a doctorate in law from Northwestern University's Pritzker School of Law. She was serving her second term as a council member when she was elected as mayor, indicating that in smaller cities and towns, even without large Muslim populations, it is possible for a Muslim American to get elected

Beyond the local level, state governments have seen a surge of Muslim Americans winning elective office. In 2019 four Muslim women in Virginia, Maine, and Minnesota were elected to their state legislatures. Ghazala Hashmi became the first Muslim to be elected to the Virginia State Senate, after upsetting a Republican incumbent. Hashmi says that when she heard about the Muslim ban, she decided, "I could continue to be quiet and accept things, or I really had to become much more visible." Thanking her supporters at her victory party, she said, "You've proven that Ghazala is truly an American name."[45]

> "I could continue to be quiet and accept things, or I really had to become much more visible."[45]
>
> —Ghazala Hashmi, Virginia state senator

On the federal level, in 2018 Representatives Ilhan Omar of Minnesota and Rashida Tlaib of Michigan became the first Muslim women elected to Congress. Omar, a Muslim who immigrated from Somalia, won in a district that was predominately white and 70 percent Christian, showing that her ethnicity and religion did not affect her ability to get elected. She replaced Keith Ellison, who had been the first Muslim person ever elected to Congress. After Congress, Ellison went on to become the state's attorney general. Since entering Congress, Omar has opposed the immigration policies that focus on limiting people entering from Muslim countries, advocated for universal health care, and supported student loan debt forgiveness. Tlaib has also supported

Rep. Ilhan Omar of Minnesota (standing, left) and Rep. Rashida Tlaib of Michigan (standing, right) await the start of the president's 2020 State of the Union address. Omar and Tlaib are the first Muslim women elected to Congress.

universal health care and a higher minimum wage. Both have become well known as progressive Democrats, and at times Trump has targeted them with derogatory comments. For instance, in 2019 he was referring to Tlaib and Omar when he tweeted, "Why don't they go back and help fix the totally broken and crime infested places from which they came."[46] As it happens, Tlaib was born in the United States and Omar is a naturalized citizen.

Positive and Negative Reactions

For Muslim Americans, seeing people like them serving in government is empowering. It shows that there is support in the public for them. Despite rhetoric against them, Muslim Americans have been elected as representatives because many Americans are looking past religion and voting for a candidate who represents their views. Suman Raghunathan, the executive director of advocacy group South Asian Americans Leading Together, says, "It's incredibly inspiring . . . to see the nation's first Muslim American women elected to Congress just two years after the administration decided to introduce the first 'Muslim ban'—I think that's a very strong, powerful message of repudiation against the politics of division rather than the politics of inclusion."[47]

However, not all have reacted positively to those of the Islamic faith making strides in government. Some have vilified the Muslim American congresswomen, depicting them as un-American and even as terrorists. Patrick W. Carlineo Jr., a New York man, threatened to kill Omar in a call to her office in 2019. In 2020 he was sentenced to a year and a day in prison. But Muslim Americans do not let such incidents deter them, and they continue to be a voice in the government.

In the Public Light

Despite backlash from people like Carlineo, Muslim Americans are changing national perceptions of themselves. Many Muslim Americans are becoming well known in areas such as entertainment and sports, bringing the spotlight to this rather hidden minority. As these popular cultural figures take the stage, more Americans realize that Muslims are people like themselves, with similar goals, interests, and hopes. Additionally, these Muslim Americans are able to educate others about their religion and dispel misconceptions.

Musa Sulaiman uses humor to challenge people's stereotypes of Muslim Americans. Sulaiman is a comedian who started the Super Muslim Comedy Tour, which has appeared across the United States and in other nations with a lineup of all Muslim American comedians. His audiences include people of all faiths. Sulaiman explains that as a black Muslim comedian, he uses comedy to make people think while laughing. Sulaiman says that his comedy builds bridges between the Muslim and non-Muslim community. "It's about going into public places and subverting the stereotypes by making people laugh," Sulaiman explains.

America's Islamic Heritage Museum

Muslim Americans believe that sharing their religion and heritage will help other Americans appreciate and understand it better. In 2011 America's Islamic Heritage Museum opened in Washington, DC, focusing on the history of Muslims in America and their varied backgrounds. The museum began in 1996 as a traveling exhibit called the Collections & Stories of American Muslims, Inc. (CSAM). It increased in popularity to the point that CSAM developers decided to establish a permanent museum.

In Washington, DC, visitors to the museum can view a timeline that begins in the 1500s and concludes in the twenty-first century, exploring the contributions of American Muslims and their legacies. It explores the different ethnic backgrounds of American Muslims and how they arrived in the United States. There is a section focusing on the Nation of Islam, an African American–based Islamic religious and political movement founded in 1930, that includes old newspaper articles, photographs, and other related memorabilia. The goal is to reach out to visitors and educate them on the different experiences of Muslim Americans and how they are an integral part of US history.

"Art and entertainment can combat ideologies of racism and bigotry."[48]

Movies and television are other entertainment areas in which Muslim Americans are making inroads. Mahershala Ali was raised as a Christian but converted to Islam as a young adult. In 2017 he became the first Muslim American to win an Academy Award, for Best Supporting Actor in *Moonlight*, and he repeated this feat in 2019 as Best Supporting Actor in *Green Book*. He is also a rapper and television actor and is well known by many audiences. To Yasmine Ghanem, a Muslim American reporter, Ali's popularity shows that more Americans are becoming accepting of Muslim Americans. "This Black-Muslim man poured his heart into

> "Art and entertainment can combat ideologies of racism and bigotry."[48]
>
> —Musa Sulaiman, comedian

his work and showed what can be done when you're given a chance," Ghanem writes. "His win showed the support we as Muslims in America actually have, even though it may be clouded by the hate of the misguided few."[49]

Also, shows featuring Muslim Americans and centering on Muslim Americans' lives are helping others understand what is like to be a Muslim in the United States. Aziz Ansari's Netflix series *Master of None* is a semiautobiographical story that explores the life of a first-generation Muslim family. Similarly, *Ramy*, a show on Hulu, follows the main character as he deals with the challenges of being an American Muslim living in post-9/11 America. Ramy Youssef, who plays himself in the show that loosely follows his life, won a Golden Globe Award for Best Actor in a comedy or musical television series in 2020. The show addresses topics like sex and dating in the Muslim community, which are

Muslim Americans are making inroads in movies, television, and other areas of entertainment. Mahershala Ali, who is Muslim, is shown celebrating his 2017 Academy Award for Best Supporting Actor in *Moonlight*.

often not discussed publicly. Jac Kern, a television critic, writes, "While very specific to Youssef's life, the story has so many facets that are relatable to many, particularly the quarter-life crisis of wondering what, where and who you're supposed to be. Add conflicting input from happy-go-lucky friends and meddling family and you're bound to feel even more lost."[50] Like Kern, many non-Muslim Americans can relate to the everyday life challenges that Youssef undergoes in the show and, at the same time, learn more about the specific difficulties of being a Muslim American.

Outside of the entertainment industry, Muslim Americans are becoming more known in the sports world. Ibtihaj Muhammad made history in 2016 when she competed in the Olympics wearing a hijab and won a medal. Muhammad represented the United States in the 2016 Summer Games in Rio and brought home a bronze medal as part of the team sabre event. She was named one of *Time* magazine's most influential people that year. Muhammad says that she fought against discrimination and stereotypes growing up but kept her focus on her sport to achieve her goals. She uses her fame to speak out against bias and encourages others to do so.

Combating Bias

Muslim Americans not in the public eye are also combating Islamophobia. Individuals are finding their own ways to eradicate discrimination. Several Muslim American organizations give advice on how individuals can repudiate bias. They believe that the way Muslim Americans respond to negative views can change these perspectives.

As an example, CAIR provides an online tool kit for Muslim Americans to work against prejudices. For example, it suggests being a good neighbor to others not of the same faith by introducing themselves and inviting their neighbors over for social occasions. Another suggestion is to involve themselves in community activities, such as the PTA at their child's school, to get to know other parents of all backgrounds. The Pew Research Center supports the idea that being a good neighbor can change biased

Protesting for Peace

Muslim Americans and their supporters are also sharing their voices through peaceful protests. The year 2020 marked the eighth annual occurrence of World Hijab Day. Nazma Khan, of the Bronx in New York City, founded the event in 2013. In her words, the event seeks to "foster religious tolerance and understanding by inviting women (non-hijabi Muslims/non-Muslims) to experience the hijab for one day." Khan came to this country from Bangladesh at age eleven. She remembers being the only girl wearing a hijab in her Bronx middle school. She remembers a lot of negative comments from other students, but she continued to wear it.

As an adult, she believes that one way to get others to understand how it feels to be targeted for wearing a hijab is to experience wearing one and learn about its meaning. Her goals are to educate women that Muslim women choose to wear the hijab to honor their religion and to counteract the idea that the hijab is to show submissiveness or oppression. On World Hijab Day, women attend events around the world, wear the hijab, and post photos of support on social media. Today it is estimated that people in 190 countries take part in World Hijab Day every year.

Quoted in World Hijab Day, "About Us," 2020. https://worldhijabday.com.

---

views. A 2017 survey found that 55 percent of non-Muslim Americans who personally know someone who is Muslim express more positive views of Muslims and Islam than do those who say they do not personally know someone who is Muslim.

Additionally, CAIR recommends that Muslim Americans act calmly, even when confronted with bigotry. "The best thing I could always suggest to an individual is to act by example. Their example must be one that is calm and collected," says Asad Ba-Yunus, a representative of the Islamic Leadership Council of New York. "Reflect the teachings of Prophet Mohammad—even in the face of his greatest enemies and critics and people who threw garbage on him, he treated people with the utmost respect and dignity."[51]

While it might not seem fair for Muslims to be urged to react calmly to discrimination, CAIR suggests that responding with facts in a calm way will help change others' stereotypes. However, CAIR also highly suggests that Muslims report incidents to authorities if they are targeted with an Islamophobic act or crime.

Many Muslim American organizations are combating bias through advocating for legislation that counters discrimination. In 2019 the fifth annual National Muslim Advocacy Day was held on Capitol Hill. On this day, national, state, and local Muslim organizations and community members come together and connect with their congressional representatives. At this event, they lobby for causes that are important to their communities. As an example, participants advocate for issues such as civil rights for all, reduction of hate crimes, and immigration reform regarding primarily Muslim countries. One political issue these groups are targeting is the addition of countries to the Muslim ban. In January 2020 the Trump administration added six countries to the ban—Eritrea, Kyrgyzstan, Myanmar, Nigeria, Sudan, and Tanzania—all with significant Muslim populations. Muslim advocacy groups protested against this expansion and continue various efforts to persuade representatives to stand against the initial ban.

Sharing Culture

Muslim Americans are also finding ways to fight against bias. One is to share their religious culture with non-Muslims. This allows non-Muslims to better understand Islam and what it really stands for, instead of believing the extremist version expressed by terrorists.

As an example, the Islamic Networks Group is a peace-building organization that provides presentations in high schools, in colleges, and at civic group meetings to foster better understanding of Muslims. Since 1993 the group has reached millions of individuals and hundreds of groups with presentations, training seminars, and workshops. One aspect of the program involves training Muslim American youth so that they can give presentations to peer groups.

One teacher comments, "This program allowed my students to learn about Islam and to hear about its history and practices from a peer which is always more powerful than hearing it from their teacher. This program also enabled my students to see Islam in a much more personal light rather than something foreign or non-applicable to their lives."[52]

Proud to Be Muslim

Muslim Americans take pride in being both American and Muslim. They do not see the two as conflicting. Like other Americans, their nationality blends with their faith to define their life, values, and culture. And, also like other Americans, they do not wish to live in fear. Rather, they fight bias by proudly being who they are and refusing to give in to fear.

Growing up in the US Midwest, Dilshad Ali practiced her Muslim faith quietly. She knew very few women who wore the hijab.

Just like young people of other faiths and other backgrounds, young Americans who follow Islam will continue to work toward achieving their dreams. When they see bias, they will call it out, but they will not let it get in their way.

Her family completed their prayers in their homes, and while they maintained Muslim practices, it was not out in the open. Now a managing editor at the religion website Patheos, Ali raises her children differently, as do many other parents of her generation. Her daughter takes a prayer mat to school for the prayer times that occur when she is there. Her nieces are part of the Muslim Students Association at their school. Ali writes:

> It's different today. I am teaching my children to be unapologetically Muslim and American. That they have as much right to be who they are outwardly and inwardly as anyone else in this country. That they are responsible for themselves and to be good citizens and human beings of this country and this earth. That they do not need to be apologetic for whatever evils and transgressions others may commit in their cruel twisting of the Muslim faith.[53]

Growing up, Taqwa Shammet was more outward than Ali with her Muslim faith, but she suffered the consequences. Shammet remembers walking the hallways of middle school in 2013 and a boy asking her if Osama bin Laden orchestrated 9/11 to honor her, since she was Muslim. She grew up hearing ignorant and negative comments like that. However, these did not stop her from growing up to be a proud Muslim American. She wore and continues to wear her hijab because it gives her peace, despite any negative comments. She writes about her pride so that others can understand what being Muslim means to her. "I was born in this country. I was born on Sept. 11, 2000. No, Osama Bin Laden did not do it to honor me. No, I'm not a terrorist. No, I don't hate my religion. No, I was not forced to wear my hijab. No, I'm not embarrassed of my religion. I am an American. I am Muslim. I am a Muslim-American. And I'm proud of it."[54]

> "I am teaching my children to be unapologetically Muslim and American."[53]
>
> —Dilshad Ali, managing editor at Patheos

SOURCE NOTES

Introduction: Thriving Against the Odds

1. Quoted in Kate Irby, "She Said 'We're Going to Kill' All Muslims in a Walmart Parking Lot. Now She's Fired," *Miami Herald*, July 27, 2017. www.miamiherald.com.
2. Quoted in Irby, "She Said 'We're Going to Kill' All Muslims in a Walmart Parking Lot."
3. Quoted in *Fort Myers (FL) News Press*, "Priest Apologizes for Calling Muslims a 'Threat' in Sermon," January 31, 2020, p. 2A.
4. Quoted in Kim Hyatt, "She Was Fired for an Anti-Muslim Tirade Toward 3 Somali Women. Now, They Plan to Help Her Get Re-Hired," *Grand Forks (ND) Herald*, July 27, 2017. www.grandforksherald.com.

Chapter One: Islamophobia on the Rise

5. Quoted in Nara Schoenberg, "6 Women: What Muslim Headscarf Means for Me," *Chicago Tribune*. http://digitaledition.chicagotribune.com.
6. Dean Obeidallah, "This Is Life for Muslim-Americans 18 Years After 9/11," *Daily Beast*, September 12, 2019. www.thedailybeast.com.
7. Quoted in Jim Key, "Three Years into His Presidency, What's the Impact of Trump's Anti-Muslim Actions?," USCDornsife, January 15, 2020. https://dornsife.usc.edu.
8. Bisma Parvez, "Muslims in America Are Just as American as Everyone Else—and We're Afraid Too," *HuffPost*, February 21, 2018. www.huffpost.com.
9. Parvez, "Muslims in America Are Just as American as Everyone Else—and We're Afraid Too."
10. Quoted in Southern Poverty Law Center, "Act for America." www.splcenter.org.

11. Mubeen Shakir, "Living with Fear as a Muslim in America," *Raleigh (NC) News & Observer*, December 14, 2015. www.newsobserver.com.
12. Quoted in Sam Levin, "Hate Crimes and Attacks Against Muslims Doubled in California Last Year—Report," *The Guardian* (Manchester), July 28, 2016. www.guardian.com.
13. Quoted in CBS News, "Chicken Express Employee Says She Was Told to Leave Because of Her Hijab," January 3, 2020. www.cbsnews.com.
14. Quoted in Leila Fadel, "Muslims in America: Telling Your Own Stories," NPR, April 20, 2018. www.npr.org.

Chapter Two: Growing Up Muslim

15. Quoted in Farida Jhabvala Romero, "Supporting Muslim Teens in Face of Islamophobia—in Their Own Schools," KQED, October 7, 2019. www.kqed.org.
16. Mansoor Shams, "My 12-Year Old Son Gave Me a List of Islamophobic Names He's Been Called," *Newsweek*, May 30, 2019. www.newsweek.com.
17. Quoted Brenda Gazzaar, "Muslim Student Claims Discrimination from South Bay Teacher," *Los Angeles Daily News*, November 10, 2015. www.dailynews.com.
18. Quoted in Lauren Talerico, "Family Upset After Teacher Allegedly Calls Student 'a Terrorist,'" KHOU, April 1, 2016. www.khou.com.
19. Quoted in Anne Runkle, "Oakland County School Districts Defend Cultural Training Despite Accusation of Pro-Muslim Bias," *Oakland Press* (Oakland County, MI), October 14, 2019. www.theoaklandpress.com.
20. Jinnie Spiegler and Sarah Sisaye, "Protecting Our Muslim Youth from Bullying: The Role of the Educator," US Department of Education, February 11, 2016. https://blog.ed.gov.
21. Quoted in Yaasameen Al-Hamdani, "Islamophobia and the Young Muslim American Experience," Middle Tennessee State University, 2016. https://jewlscholar.mtsu.edu.
22. Hana Alasry, "I'm Embarrassed to Pray in Public," About Islam, September 3, 2019. https://aboutislam.net.

23. Quoted in Al-Hamdani, "Islamophobia and the Young Muslim American Experience."
24. Quoted in Kirk Semple, "Young Muslim Americans Are Feeling the Strain of Suspicion," *New York Times*, December 15, 2015. www.nytimes.com.
25. Quoted in C.J. Werleman, "Trump Has Led the Way for Schoolyard Bullying of American Muslims," Middle East Eye, January 4, 2018. www.middleeasteye.net.
26. Quoted in Semple, "Young Muslim Americans Are Feeling the Strain of Suspicion."
27. Quoted in Romero, "Supporting Muslim Teens in Face of Islamophobia—in Their Own Schools."
28. Quoted in Romero, "Supporting Muslim Teens in Face of Islamophobia—in Their Own Schools."

Chapter Three: Hate Crimes

29. Quoted in Tanvi Misra, "United States of Anti-Muslim Hate," CityLab, March 9, 2018. www.citylab.com.
30. Quoted in Francesca Paris, "Militia Members Plead Guilty to 2017 Minnesota Mosque Bombing," NPR, January 24, 2019. www.npr.org.
31. Quoted in *Victoria (TX) Advocate*, "Update: Arsonist Marq Vincent Perez Gets 24-Year Federal Prison Sentence," October 7, 2018. www.victoriaadvocate.com.
32. Quoted in *Victoria (TX) Advocate*, "Update."
33. Quoted in Amr Alfiky and Adeel Hasaan, "'Make Sure Not to Talk Any Arabic': American Muslims and Their Guns," *New York Times*, June 7, 2018. www.nytimes.com.
34. Quoted in Greg Garrison, "In Face of Threats, Alabama Muslims Receive Support, Welcome Visitors," AL.com, February 20, 2017. www.al.com.
35. Quoted in Christine Hauser, "Texas Mosque Gutted by Mysterious Blaze Raises More than $900,000 to Rebuild," *New York Times*, January 30, 2017. www.nytimes.com.

Chapter Four: Political Impacts

36. Farhana Khera, "Reform the Un-American Patriot Act," October 26, 2011. www.cnn.com.

37. Quoted in Theodore Schleifer, "I Think 'Islam' Hates Us," CNN, March 3, 2016. www.cnn.com.
38. Quoted in Clare Foran, "Donald Trump and the Rise of Anti-Muslim Violence," *The Atlantic*, September 22, 2016. www.theatlantic.com.
39. Aziz Ansari, "Why Trump Makes Me Scared for My Family," *New York Times*, June 6, 2016. www.nytimes.com.
40. Jennifer Mayers, "I Support the Muslim Ban: A Christian Mother Speaks," *It's a Jenn Thing: Ponder This* (blog), January 1, 2017. https:jennifermayers.wordpress.com.
41. Quoted in *The Guardian* (Manchester), "Muslim Americans on Trump's Travel Ban: 'We Live as Second-Class Citizens,'" June 26, 2018. www.theguardian.com.
42. Quoted in India West, "Arkansas Senator Jason Rapert's Twitter Account Temporarily Suspended," December 13, 2019. www.indiawest.com.
43. Quoted in Gus Burns, "Battle over Michigan Mosque Rages On in Lawsuit Citing ISIS Violence," MLive, March 16, 2017. www.mlive.com.
44. Quoted in Daniel Victor, "Muslim Group Wins Right to Build Mosque in Michigan City," *New York Times*, February 22, 2017. www.nytimes.com.

Chapter Five: Finding Their Place

45. Quoted in Sarah Mervosh, "She Doubted Her Place in America. Now She's Virginia's First Muslim State Senator," *New York Times*, November 6, 2019. www.nytimes.com.
46. Quoted in Bianca Quilantan and David Cohen, "Trump Tells Dem Congresswomen: Go Back Where You Came From," *Politico*, July 14, 2019. www.politico.com.
47. Quoted in Tara Burton, "Tlaib and Omar Are the First Muslim Women Elected to Congress. They're Also So Much More," Vox, November 8, 2018. www.vox.com.
48. Quoted in Kim Hjelmgaard, "What You Don't Know About America's Islamic Heritage," *USA Today*, November 18, 2018. www.usatoday.com.

49. Yasmine Ghanem, "As a Muslim, Watching Mahershala Ali Win an Oscar Gave Me Hope," The Tab, February 28, 2017. https://thetab.com.
50. Jac Kern, "Hulu's Groundbreaking *Ramy* Brings Laughs and Lessons," CityBeat, May 17, 2019. www.citybeat.com.
51. Quoted in CAIR, "Anti-Prejudice Tools," May 13, 2019. www.islamophobia.org.
52. Quoted in ING, "ING Youth Testimonials," 2020. https://ing.org.
53. Dilshad Ali, "What Does Being 'Unapologetically Muslim' Mean?," Patheos, March 17, 2018. www.patheos.com.
54. Tagwa Shammet, "I Am a Proud Muslim American," *Commonwealth Times*, March 27, 2019. https://commonwealthtimes.org.

ORGANIZATIONS AND WEBSITES

American Muslim Council
www.muslimcouncilofamerica.org

A nonprofit organization, the American Muslim Council is dedicated to tackling issues such as discrimination, poverty, and civil rights. It seeks to connect Muslim Americans with all Americans. Its website provides information on the beliefs of Islam, Muslim American issues, and community services the organization provides.

Council on American-Islamic Relations (CAIR)
www.cair.com

CAIR is a nonprofit organization and the largest Muslim civil liberties organization in the United States. It is focused on ensuring that the Muslim American voice is heard using media relations, lobbying, education, and advocacy. Its website provides a list of projects it is involved in, events it sponsors, and civil rights reports.

Islamic Circle of North America (ICNA) — www.icna.org

The ICNA is focused on helping Muslim Americans adhere to Islamic values while living in religiously diverse communities. It helps provide and maintain connections between Muslim Americans and their faith. The ICNA website provides information on its outreach programs and social services.

Islamic Society of North America (ISNA) — www.isna.net

The mission of the ISNA is to help develop unity in the Muslim American community, support interfaith relations, engage civically, and promote a better understanding of Islam. Its website includes an online magazine about its events and projects, information on events throughout the country, and news about its annual convention.

Muslim Students Association (MSA) National

www.msanational.org

MSA National is meant to unite Muslim American youth and empower them to be good citizens in their communities. The association has chapters at schools throughout the nation, focused on helping students practice their faith, connect with one another, and engage in the community. Its website includes guiding principles and webinars on issues pertinent to Muslim American youth.

FOR FURTHER RESEARCH

Books

Sumbul Ali-Karamali, *Demystifying Shariah: What It Is, How It Works, and Why It's Not Taking Over Our Country*. Boston: Beacon, 2020.

Shabana Mir, *Muslim American Women on Campus: Undergraduate Social Life and Identity*. Chapel Hill: University of North Carolina Press, 2016.

Next Wave Muslim Initiative Writers, *I Am the Night Sky & Other Reflections by Muslim American Youth*. Washington, DC: Shout Mouse, 2019.

Sabeeha Rehman, *Threading My Prayer Rug: One Woman's Journey from Pakistani Muslim to American Muslim*. New York: Arcade, 2017.

Ayser Salman, *The Wrong End of the Table: A Mostly Comic Memoir of a Muslim American Woman Just Trying to Fit In*. New York: Skyhorse, 2019.

Internet Sources

Isaac Chotiner, "How Muslim Americans Are Viewed in the Trump Era," Slate, June 21, 2018. https://slate.com.

Leila Fadel, "America's Next Generation of Muslims Insists on Crafting Its Own Story," NPR, April 12, 2018. www.npr.org.

Shadi Hamid, "For Religious American Muslims, Hostility from the Right and Disdain from the Left," *Order from Chaos* (blog), Brookings Institution, August 5, 2109. www.brookings.edu.

Dean Obeidallah, "This Is Life for Muslim Americans, 18 Years After 9-11," Daily Beast, September 12, 2019. www.thedailybeast.com.

Gabriel Sanchez, "This Is What Muslim American Youth Looks like in New York," BuzzFeed, November 24, 2016. www.buzzfeed.com.

INDEX

Note: Boldface page numbers indicate illustrations.

Abercrombie & Fitch, **19**, 20
Abushaaban, Waleed, 25–26
Act! for America, 14, 18
Afghanistan, war in, 43–44, **44**
Ajrami, Abe, 42
Alang, Sirry, 30
alarm clock "bomb" incident, 27
Alasry, Hana, 29
Albeshari, Rasheed, 19
Ali, Dilshad, 63
Ali, Mahershala, 58, **59**
Ali, Sumaya, 24
Allen, Curtis, 36–37
Almiggabber, Zayneb, 30–31
al Qaeda, 15–16, 43
Alsultany, Evelyn, 14–15
American Islamic Community Center (Sterling Heights, Michigan), 52–53
American Jewish Committee, 35
American Journal of Public Health, 34
American Muslim Council, 70
American Muslim Institution, 45
Ansari, Aziz, 46–47, 59
Ansary, Nadia, 31
Anti-Defamation League, 16
anti-Muslim organizations, 14, 18–19
anti-Muslim speech
  hate crimes correlation to, 46
  by Republicans, 45, 51–52
  by Trump, 35, 45, 46–47, **47**
Applebee's incident, 32–33, **33**
Arain, Zainab, 14

Ba Yunus, Asad, 61–62
bin Laden, Osama, 15–16
Bloomington, Minnesota, mosque attacked in, 36–38, **41**
Boston Marathon bombing, 16
Brennan Center for Justice, 49–50
bullying
  learning how to deal with, 31
  in school, 21–23, 26
Bureau of Alcohol, Tobacco, Firearms and Explosives, 17
Bush, George W., 43
BuzzFeed News, 52

California State University, San Bernardino, 46
Cambridge, Massachusetts, mayor of, 55
Campbell, Jasmine Renee, 39–40
Carlineo, Patrick W., Jr., 57
Center for American Progress, 18
Center for the Study of Hate and Extremism (California State University, San Bernardino), 46
Chandler, Paul, 17
Chicken Express, 20
Chowdhury, Helal, 24
Civil Rights Act (1964), 17
clothing of women
  discrimination and, 6, 10, **19**, 20, 39–40
  in sports, 60
  World Hijab Day, 61
CNN poll, 48
Coleman, Stefanae, 20
community support
  after attacks on mosques, 35, **41**, 42
  after threats to Islamic centers, 41–42
  percentage of Muslims who have had support expressed by non-Muslims, 9

74

Council on American-Islamic Relations (CAIR)
   advice on behavior when facing discrimination and bias, 61–62
   basic information about, 70
   charity funding of anti-Muslim organizations, 14
   number of anti-Muslim hate crimes in California (2014–2015), 19
   number of occurrences of anti-Muslim bias (2014–2019), 8
   online tool kit for fighting discrimination, 60
   percentage of Muslim children bullied or abused in school, 21
Crusaders, 36–37
Culpeper County, Virginia, 52

Dar Al-Farooq Islamic Center (Bloomington, Minnesota), 36–38, **41**
de Blasio, Bill, 24
discrimination
   bullying, harassment, and violence in school, 21–23, 26
   clothing and
     of men, 33
     of women, 6, 10, **19**, 20, 39–40
   in daily life, 29–31, 61–62
   dealing with, **19**, 20
   fear as cause of, 18–19
   levels of, against Muslim, Jews, and evangelical Christians, **13**
   number of occurrences of anti-Muslim bias (2014–2019), 8
   organizations combating, 61–63, 70–71
     See also Council on American-Islamic Relations (CAIR)
   percentage of Muslims whom experienced, 8
   perception of, 8
   as systemic, 43
   while shopping, 28
   in workplace, **19**, 20
   See also hate crimes

East Brunswick High School (New Jersey), 22–23
Eid al-Adha, 24
Eid al-Fitr, 24
Elauf, Majda, **19**
Elauf, Samantha, **19**, 20
Elder, Azzam, 53
Elkabti, Fatima, 20
Ellison, Keith, 55
entertainment, Muslims in, 46–47, 57–60, **59**
Essa, Huda, 26

FBI
   number of anti-Muslim hate crimes (2000–2001), 17
   number of anti-Muslim hate crimes (2018), 35
   searches by, 44
fears of Muslim Americans
   of attacks on individuals, 39–40
   of attacks on mosques, 38
   as being racially profiled and targeted by FBI, 44
   in everyday life, 18
   guns for protection, 40
   level of, 12
   of Muslim extremists, 15
   stress from, 29–31
   threats made against, 39, 41, 57
   Trump and, 46–47
Fidelity Charitable, 14
Fort Bend, Texas, 25–26
Fort Myers, Florida, 39

Gabriel, Brigitte, 18
Ghanem, Yasmine, 58–59
government, Muslims in, 55–57, **56**
Gretel, Mike, 53
gun ownership, 17, 40

Halal Meat and Grocery Store (Fort Myers, Florida), 39
Hamdani, Yaasameen Al-, 28
Hari, Michael, 36
Hashmi, Ghazala, 55
Hashmi, Shahid, 38
Hassan, Abdullah, 51
Hassan, Ali, 51
Hassan, Leyla, **7**

Hassan, Sarah, 6, **7**, 9
hate crimes
  as cyclical, 34–35
  harassment, 19–20
  hateful speech versus, 38
  number of anti-Muslim
    2000–2001, 17
    2018, 35
    in California (2014–2015), 19
    increase in, after September 11 attacks, 16–18, 34
    increase in, after Trump's anti-Muslim rhetoric, 46
  protection against, 40
  state laws, 40
  violent
    attacks on mosques, 35, 36–38, **37**
    threats of, against Muslim businesses, 39
    threats of, against Muslim individuals, 33–34, 39–40, 41, 57
health issues from stress, 30
Hensley, Amber Elizabeth, 6, **7**, 9
hijab, 10

Institute for Social Policy and Understanding
  ethnic and racial makeup of Muslims, 8
  level of fear of Muslims in America, 12
  percentage of Muslim children bullied in school, 21
Irving Independent School District (Texas), 27
Islam
  basic information about, 6–7
  extremist
    beliefs of, 12
    global jihad by, 16
    percentage of American Muslims worried about, 15
    terrorism and, 10–11, **11**, 15–16
  non-Muslim Americans having negative views of, 15, 45
  See also anti-Muslim speech
  pride in, 64
  religious practice, **28**, 28–29
Islam, Md, 39
Islamic Center (Victoria, Texas), 37, **37**, 42
Islamic Center of Culpeper (Virginia), 52
Islamic Circle of North America (ICNA), 70
Islamic Heritage Museum, 58
Islamic Networks Group, 31, 62–63
Islamic Society of Greater Worcester, 50
Islamic Society of North America, 35, 70–71
Islamophobia
  funded by charities, 14
  gun sales to Muslims and, 17
  increase in, since September 11, 2001, 10
  level of, in US, 12
  opposition to building of mosques, 52–53
  percentage of Americans having negative views of, 15, 45
  refusal to allow Muslim cemetery, 50
  sources of, 10–11, **11**, 14–16
  See also anti-Muslim speech; discrimination
"Islamophobia and the Young American Experience" (Hamdani), 28

Jama, Asma, 32–33, **33**
Jamal, Hebh, 29–30
Jennings, Craig, 17
Jewish-Muslim bond, 35, 42
Jones, James Benjamin, 39

Kern, Jac, 60
Khan, Nazma, 61
Khera, Farhana, 44

Lara, Julius, 39
Leadership Conference on Civil and Human Rights, 40

76

Leuzinger High School (Lawndale, California), 24
Lizotte, Jeffrey, 17

Master of None (television program), 59
Matthews, Steve, 26
Mayers, Jennifer, 49
McKenzie, Robert, 35
McWhorter, Michael, 36
Minneapolis, Minnesota, 32–34, **33**
Mohamed, Ahmed, 27
Morris, Joe, 36
Muhammad (Prophet), 7, 12
Muhammad, Ibtihaj, 60
Muslim Advocates, 40, 44
Muslim-Jewish Advisory Council, 35
Muslim Students Association (MSA) National, 64, 71

NAACP Legal Defense and Educational Fund, 40
National Muslim Advocacy Day, 62
National Security Letters, 44
NBC/*Wall Street Journal* poll, 48
New America, 35, 45
New York City, 24
New Zealand, mosque attacked in, 35

Oakland County, Michigan school system, 26
Obama, Barack, 27
Obeidallah, Dean, 13
Omar, Ilhan, 55–56, **56**, 57
Omeish, Abrar, 49

Parvez, Bisma, 15, 16
Pathan, Ishaq, 31
Patriot Act, 44
Perez, Marq Vincent, 37
Pew Research Center
　correlation between knowing Muslims and having positive views, 60–61
　levels of discrimination against Muslim, Jews, and evangelical Christians, **13**

Muslim population in US, 6, 7
　percentage experiencing discrimination regularly, 8
　percentage increase in anti-Muslim incidents (2014–206), 34
　percentage of American Muslims worried about extremist Muslims, 15
　percentage of Americans having negative views about Islam, 15, 45
　percentage of Muslims proud to be American, 8
　percentage of Muslims who believe Americans are generally friendly, 9
　percentage of Muslims who have had support expressed by non-Muslims, 9
　percentage of support for Islamist extremism among Muslim Americans, 12
political office, Muslims holding, 55–57, **56**
population in US
　ethnic and racial groups, 8
　number of adults, 7
　number of Muslim Americans under eighteen, 21
　number of total Muslims, 6
　percentage of immigrants, 7
prejudice. *See* discrimination

Raghunathan, Suman, 56–57
Rainey, John, 37
Ramy (television program), 59–60
Rapert, Jason, 51–52
Republicans and rhetoric about Muslims, 45
　See also anti-Muslim rhetoric by *under* Trump, Donald

Sadozai, Khalid, 50
Sahara Mediterranean Market (Fort Myers, Florida), 39
San Bernardino, California, shooting, 16, 19, 32
Sawina, Anthony, 33–34

school
    anti-bias programs in, 26–27, 62–63
    attitudes of teachers, 23–26, 63
    calendar, religious holidays on, 24
    bullying in, 21–23, 26
    Muslim Students Associations, 64, 71
    violence in, 22–23
Schwab, 14
September 11, 2001 terrorist attacks, 10–11, **11**, 16–18, 34
Shakir, Mubeen, 18
Shammet, Tagwa, 64
Shams, Mansoor, 23
sharia law, 12, 18
Shibly, Hassan, 40
Shohoud, Sara, 23
Siddiqui, Sumbul, 55
Sikh Coalition, 40
Slader, Denise, 19–20
Smith, Syend, 39
Somali Muslim community in Minneapolis, Minnesota, **33**, 32–34
Southern Poverty Law Center, 18
Soyan, Rowda, 6, 8
speech, freedom of, 38
Spiegler, Jinnie, 27
sports, Muslims in, 60
Stein, Patrick Eugene, 36–37
Stengel, Richard, 38
Sterling Heights, Michigan, 52–53
stress, 29–31
Sulaiman, Musa, 57–58
Supreme Court, travel ban decision by, 48
Swileh, Shaima, 50–51

Taufique, Ashfaq, 41–42
Teach Us Your Name (Essa), 26
terrorism, 10–11, **11**, 15–16
Time (magazine), 60
Tlaib, Rashida, 55–56, **56**

Todd, David, **7**, 9
travel ban on entrance of Muslims into US
    effect of, 49–51
    opposition to, **48**, 62
    Supreme Court decision about, 48
    as Trump campaign proposal, 45, 46, **47**
    as Trump executive order, 47–48
Tree of Life synagogue (Pittsburgh, Pennsylvania), 35
Trump, Donald
    anti-Muslim rhetoric by, 35, 45, 46–47, **47**
    derogatory comments about Tlaib and Omar, 55–56
    travel ban on entrance of Muslims into US
    effect of, 49–51
    opposition to, **48**, 62
    as Trump campaign proposal, 45, 46, **47**
    as Trump executive order, 47–48

Union for Reform Judaism, 40
US Department of Education (DOE), anti-bullying guidance from, 26–27
US Supreme Court, **19**, 20, 48

Valeski, Victor, 22, 23
vandalism, 32–33
VanDenBroeke, Nick, 8
Victoria, Texas, mosque attacked in, 37, **37**, 42

Worcester, Massachusetts, cemetery application, 50
World Hijab Day, 61
Wright, Gavin, 36–37

Youssef, Ramy, 59–60
Youth Speakers Training, 31

PICTURE CREDITS

Cover: LeoPatrizi/iStockphoto

7: Associated Press
11: Dan Howell/Shutterstock.com
13: Maury Aaseng
19: Associated Press
22: FatCamera/iStockphoto
25: © 20th Century Fox/Photofest Images
28: mustafagull/iStockphoto
33: Richard Tsong-Taatarii/Newscom
37: Associated Press
41: Associated Press
44: Associated Press
47: Brad McPherson/Shutterstock
48: Ting Shen Xinhua News Agency/Newscom
56: Associated Press
59: Tinseltown/Shutterstock
63: Rawpixel/iStockphoto

ABOUT THE AUTHOR

Leanne K. Currie-McGhee lives in Norfolk, Virginia, with her husband, two daughters, and a dog. She has written educational books for over fifteen years and enjoys continually learning.